MURDER IN THE HOUSTON HIGH RISE

TEXAS-SIZED MYSTERIES, BOOK 6

MICHELLE FRANCIK

© 2019, Michelle Francik.

All rights reserved. Except as permitted under the U.S. Copyright Act of 1976, no part of this publication may be reproduced, distributed or transmitted in any form or by any means, or stored in a database or retrieval system without the prior written permission of the publisher.

Cover Design by RockSolidBookDesign.com
Proofread by Alice Shepherd

This is a work of fiction. Names, characters, organizations, places, events, and incidents are either products of the author's imagination or are used fictitiously. Any resemblance to actual persons, living or dead, or actual events is purely coincidental.

No part of this work may be reproduced, or stored in a retrieval system, or transmitted in any form or by any means, electronic, mechanical, photocopying, recording, or otherwise, without written permission of the publisher.

SWEET PROMISE PRESS
PO BOX 72
BRIGHTON, MI 48116

What's our Sweet Promise? It's to deliver the heart-warming, entertaining, clean, and wholesome reads you love with every single book.

From contemporary to historical romances to suspense and even cozy mysteries, all of our books are guaranteed to put a song in your heart and a smile on your face. That's our promise to you, and we can't wait to deliver upon it...

We release one new book per week, which means the flow of sweet, relatable reads coming your way never ends. Make sure to save some space on your eReader!

Check out our books in Kindle Unlimited at
sweetpromisepress.com/Unlimited

———

Download our free app to keep up with the latest releases and unlock cool bonus content at sweetpromisepress.com/App

———

Join our reader discussion group, meet our authors, and make new friends at sweetpromisepress.com/Group

———

Sign up for our weekly newsletter at sweetpromisepress.com/Subscribe

———

And don't forget to like us on Facebook at sweetpromisepress.com/FB

1

A tear rolled down Ashanti Jones' face as she closed the laptop; Adam Donahue's invitation still ringing in her ears. Jayla cooed and reached for her mom's hoop earring, but she deftly shifted the baby on her hip, so the jewelry was out of reach. She reached up and wiped the tear from her cheek. She knew Adam meant well, but she didn't feel it was appropriate to stay with him in his high-rise condo in Houston. It would be him, her and her baby. She liked him—a lot. And she knew he cared for her and Jayla. She also knew how easy it was to fall into a relationship and let things go too far, too fast.

She looked down at her daughter and sighed. She was grateful she had this beautiful child in her life, but she didn't want to make the same mistake again. She needed to keep her distance from Adam until she was sure she wanted a long-term relationship with him. Then, she had to take it slow and do things the right way.

She heard a car pull up in front of the farmhouse. Two doors slammed and Susan Sinclair's laugh rang out through the chill morning air. Ashanti sighed. She was happy for her new friends, she really was. But it hurt to see how happy they were, how in love, when she was all alone. She leaned down and kissed her daughter's forehead. As if sensing her mother's odd mood, Jayla cooed and smiled, her tiny hand reaching up to grab Ashanti's nose.

"I know little one, we got each other and that's all we be needin'." She sighed as she hiked her up higher on her hip. "C'mon girl, let's put on our happy faces and go say hi."

****

"Oh my gosh! Look how big she's getting! Are you testing out Adam's new feed on her, or what?" Reed reached for Jayla who was grinning at her favorite "uncle," hands extended towards him. Ashanti handed her over with a "hmpf."

"Of course not, silly. She's just a good eater, like her mama." Ashanti posed--her hand on her ample hip and her head thrown back.

Susan laughed, walked up to her and hugged her. "How are you doing? I feel like I don't have time to talk to you, what with all the wedding preparations."

Susan and Reed's wedding was coming up and Maggie and Garrett had offered to let them have the wedding at their farm. So, the soon-to-be sisters-in-law were closeted in the office nearly every afternoon, evening and weekend, ironing out the details. Ashanti knew she was welcome to help, but she usually volunteered to watch Walker, Maggie's son, so the two women could work without distractions.

Jayla and Walker had been born a few days apart and were now three months old. They didn't do much besides eat, sleep and poop, so she had a lot of time to think.

Maggie Donahue was married to Garrett Donahue, and this was their home, Stony Gulch Farm. Maggie was a U.S. Marshal and Garrett worked the farm, which was known for its dairy, eggs, and goat hair yarn. Their son Walker was the spitting image of his dad and uncle, with blue eyes and dark, wavy hair.

Ashanti and Maggie had met in the maternity ward at Sweet Grove Community Hospital, when they'd both been about to pop. They'd solved a murder, had their babies, and become fast friends.

Susan Sinclair was about to marry Reed Donahue, Garrett's brother and Maggie's U.S. Marshal partner. Susan was a teacher at Sweet Grove Middle School. She'd met Reed and Maggie while she'd been in WITSEC, waiting to testify against a murderer.

Watching the interactions between the two couples had shown Ashanti just how dysfunctional her previous relationship had been. Jayla's father had never cherished her or gone out of his way for her, like Reed and Garrett did. Everything was always about him and what she should do to make him happy.

Her role model growing up had been her nana, and Nana had been single for a long time. Every day she threw herself into taking care of her family, giving her all to her grandchildren and asking nothing for herself. She'd taught her granddaughter to be strong and independent, but not how to have a healthy relationship.

Ashanti's grandfather had died before she was born. Her nana said he'd been the love of her life, and his death had broken her heart so bad nothing could ever fix it. Whenever she looked into her daughter's eyes, Ashanti felt like she understood. Her daughter had stolen her heart and she had no idea how she'd survive if anything happened to her.

She'd been so lost in her thoughts she hadn't heard Maggie and Garrett enter the kitchen. A hand on her arm startled her and she turned to see a silly grin on her friend's face. "What's got you so dreamy-eyed? Weren't you just talkin' to Adam on the computer?"

Ashanti felt her face grow red, but she wasn't sure if she was embarrassed or annoyed. Couldn't a woman talk to a man without everyone gettin' all goofy about it? "Actually, I was thinkin' bout how much I love my little Jayla, if you must know."

"Don't go getting' all huffy on me, missy. I was just askin'." Maggie grinned and took the cup of coffee that Garrett handed her. "Mmm, I love it when Reed makes the coffee."

"Don't you have a doctor's appointment today?" Garrett looked at his watch, then up at Ashanti. "I'll be ready to take you in about 30 minutes, if that works for you."

"Thanks, Garrett, I nearly forgot. Reed, I need my baby back." She reached for Jayla, but Reed didn't want to let go.

"She's so danged sweet, Ashanti. I think I could hold her all day long and never get bored." He placed a kiss on the tip of Jayla's nose, making the baby squeal with delight. "See! She loves her Uncle Reed, too!"

"Yes, she does. Now hand her over or I'll have Maggie shoot you."

"Hey, don't drag me into this," Maggie laughed.

"Oh, all right. Here you go." He handed her to Ashanti, then made a face. He looked down at the wet spot on his shirt. "Um, Ashanti? I think she might need a diaper change."

2
———

Dr. Rosales was looking at her intently, her brows drawn together and a frown on her lips.

"What?" Ashanti asked. "Why you lookin' at me like that?"

The doctor sighed. "Do you trust me, Ashanti?"

"I think so, why?"

"I know you say you're doing fine, but I still see signs of postpartum depression and frankly, I'm a little concerned."

She shrugged. "So what if I've got the baby blues. It's normal, ain't it?"

"Well, yes and no. Every woman experiences being a new mom differently. For some, depression sets in and becomes a problem. My concern is that you seem to be sliding in deeper, rather than improving."

Ashanti sighed and picked at some lint on her stretchy black pants. "I think it's more 'bout having to be around all the lovey-dovey stuff at the Donahue's than about postpartum." She looked up at the doctor, who nodded, encouraging her to continue.

"It's just hard. There's the wedding planning goin' on and the way those men dote on their women is so sugar sweet it's sickening. Then there's me. All alone."

Dr. Rosales grinned. "You're not alone, but I understand why you feel like you are. Have you thought about finding your own place?"

"Well, yeah, of course. But I don't have a job or skills or a babysitter or nothin'. It's kinda overwhelming, truth be told."

"Is there anywhere you could go? Even for a weekend or something? I think it would do you a world of good to have a change of scenery."

Ashanti looked down at her hands, wondering if she should mention Adam's offer.

"Out with it, Ashanti. I can see those wheels turning. What's on your mind?"

"Well, Adam offered for me and Jayla to stay with him for a few days in Houston."

"That sounds like a great idea. You'd have a whole city to explore, new people to see. I think you should go." She paused and when Ashanti continued to pick at non-existent lint, she asked, "What's the holdup?"

"I just don't know how 'propriate it is for me to stay there in his condo with him. I mean, I just don't know."

Dr. Rosales leaned forward and placed her hand on Ashanti's. "I was there when that young man stepped in and helped you through labor. I saw the look on his face when he saw Jayla, and we placed her in your arms. From what I've seen, he's a good man. I can't see him doing anything to place you in a compromising situation."

"I know all that, it's just . . ." She was uncomfortable admitting it out loud, but she was on a roll and it tumbled out. "I kinda like him and I don't want to make the same mistake I made with Jayla's biological dad."

"Well you won't. Adam is not that man. And you are no longer that woman. You're a mom and you love your daughter. You're not going to let anyone take advantage of either of you. And as I said before, he's a good man. I've met his brothers and I've seen how they treat their women with love and respect. I can't imagine he would even *think* of doing that to you."

Ashanti's eyes filled with tears and she started to sob. Jayla woke up and started to cry, too. She picked her up and held her against her chest until the two of them had cried their fill.

****

The drive back to Stony Gulch Farm was quiet, with Jayla napping and Ashanti considering everything the doctor said.

"Everythin' okay?" Garrett's voice broke into her reverie and she turned towards him, noticing the concern on his face.

"Yeah, I think so. I just got a lot on my mind."

Garrett was quiet as he turned onto the farm driveway. "You know Mags and I are always here for you. If there's anything you need, you just tell us."

Her eyes filled with tears and she realized the doctor might have a point. She wasn't one to get emotional yet here she was, blubbering for the third time in one day. "Thanks, Garrett, I know that and I 'preciate you both."

Maggie met them at the front door of the farmhouse, Walker in her arms.

"Did Susan and Reed leave already?"

"Yep. I'm feeling kinda wore out today, so I asked if I could have some time to spend with my husband." She placed her free arm around his neck and pulled his face down to hers.

Ashanti felt her eyes well up and brushed past them to get into the house. Before she could reach the safety of her room, Maggie called out to her.

"I hope you're hungry, Ashanti. Reed made some amazing blueberry muffins and Marta left you a bowl of her three-alarm chili."

"I'll be right out," she called back. She set her purse and the diaper bag on her bed, then carefully placed the sleeping Jayla in her crib. Her daughter opened her eyes, snorted, and stuck her thumb in her mouth, falling quickly back to sleep.

Ashanti stretched and groaned. Who knew carrying a three-month-old would be so hard on the back? She looked at the bed longingly, torn between taking a nap and eating lunch. Marta, the Donahue's housekeeper, made the best chili, and she was definitely hungry, so food won out. She took one last look at her daughter, then headed for the kitchen.

. . .

****

The chili had been eaten, along with a blueberry muffin chaser and Ashanti was walking back to her room to check on Jayla when she overheard a conversation between Maggie and Garrett. She hadn't intended to listen, but their voices carried from the front porch through the living room window, and she heard everything.

"You know I love helping, Garrett, but honestly, it's a lot to deal with. I miss being able to be alone with my husband. I think I might have to have a talk with her, but I don't want to hurt her feelings. I have to go back to work soon and I just want to relax and enjoy the time I have with you and Walker."

Ashanti's heart started pounding and she felt sick to her stomach. She'd never wanted to intrude on Maggie, and she'd done her best to be helpful and give her space. Apparently, it hadn't been enough. Her friend was hurting, and it was all her fault.

She hurried into her room and shut the door. Jayla was still asleep, but she picked her up and held her tight, needing the comfort of holding her in her arms. The baby opened her eyes and looked directly into her mom's. Bubbles formed at the corner of her mouth as she pursed her lips and cooed.

"I love you, too, baby girl. It's just you and me together in this world. I forgot for a moment, but now I remember. I got some thinkin' to do, but Nana didn't raise no fool." She set Jayla on the bed and stretched out next to her. *What am I going to do?*

****

When the computer dinged the next morning, announcing Adam's call, she almost didn't bother with it. She hadn't slept well, worrying about Maggie and herself and Jayla. She wanted to be proactive and have a plan in place before she talked to her friend but was at a loss about what to do.

She flipped the laptop open and grinned at the image on the screen. "Adam, you crazy."

"Haha! I know, right? What do you think of my ostrich feather? The feather in my cap, if you will."

"I don't know what that means, but that's a Stetson and even a country girl like me knows it ain't no 'cap.'" Adam was wearing his white cowboy hat and had attached a beautiful, white ostrich feather to the band. "You look kinda like one of them three musketeers, truth be told."

"Hmm. That wasn't what I was going for, but I'll

take it." He made a sweeping gesture with his arm and bowed his head. "Thank you, milady."

Ashanti chuckled. "You're a strange one, Adam Donahue."

"Again, thank you, milady," he chuckled. "How are my two favorite gals, today?"

"Jayla's growing like a weed. Yesterday Reed asked if I was feedin' her that growth stuff you been pushin' on Garrett, but I told him no, she's just a good eater like her mama."

Adam's face dropped and he removed his hat, setting it down out of sight of the camera. "I wish I could be there. I'm missing out on so much, being so far away." He paused, but she didn't know what to say, so she stayed silent.

"How's her mama doing? Are you taking care of yourself? You look a little tired."

"Now Adam, I know your mama taught you some manners. You never tell a lady she looks tired. It's rude."

"I'm sorry, Miss Thing, I wasn't trying to rile you up. I'm just worried about you, that's all."

Ashanti felt bad. She hadn't meant to rile him up, either. "I know, I guess I *am* tired and feelin' out of sorts."

"Have you thought any more about my offer?" He

looked at her, a hopeful expression on his handsome face.

"Have you been talkin' to Maggie?" She wondered, all of a sudden, if maybe they were in cahoots on trying to get her out of the farmhouse.

"No way, no how. The last time I called, I had to hear all about the wedding preparations and such. Too much information, to my way of thinkin'. Now I just communicate with Garrett via text message." He shuddered and shook his head. "I don't know why women gotta make such a huge deal out of the wedding. It's only one day. It's the rest of their life they should be focusing on. That's the part that counts."

"You shut your mouth, you. I'm back to thinkin' you're the dumb brother, just 'cause of that there statement."

Adam laughed. "You know I'm joshing you. I want a big wedding, too. I've got it all planned out. I want a white wedding. White chrysanthemums, white tablecloths, white cake with white frosting and white ostrich feathers in white vases. And of course, a bunch of rhinestones and glitter to make it all sparkle."

"You know you scare me, right?"

He laughed again. "I scare most people, but I

don't believe I scare you, Ashanti. I think you get where I'm coming from."

"Mmm. I ain't admitting nothin'." She sighed and watched his face turned serious again.

"What's going on? I can tell something's on your mind." His concern touched her, and she admitted to herself his offer might be just what she needed. If she stayed with him in the city for a few days, she could look for a job and a place to stay. The city offered more opportunities, and if she found something, he'd probably let her stay until she got on her feet. It would be good to have help with Jayla and a safe place to stay while she figured things out.

"I was thinkin' 'bout what you said; that it might do me and Jayla good to get away for a bit. But I just want to be sure that you're okay with havin' us up in your home."

"Of course, I am. I wouldn't have offered if I didn't mean it."

He looked and sounded excited and the last of her fears dissipated. "Fine then. Me and Jayla accept your kind offer."

"Woohoo!" Adam's whoop of joy rivaled the one Garrett had let out the first time she'd met him, and for a moment, the resemblance between the brothers was striking. "I can't wait to let Jayla crawl around on my leopard skin rug! It's not real leopard, you know, but it's soft and pretty and I know you'll love it!"

And there the similarity ends, she chuckled to herself.

3

*A*s they drove away from the farmhouse, Ashanti felt tears well up in her eyes. Adam reached over and patted her hand with his, keeping his eyes firmly on the road as he navigated them out to the highway.

She'd been relieved and a little excited once she'd made her decision. She worried about telling Maggie, but based on the conversation she'd overheard, she thought her friend would be thrilled. That afternoon at lunch she'd announced it to everyone.

"I was thinkin' that me and Jayla need a change, so when I spoke with Adam this mornin', I accepted his offer to visit Houston."

"That's wonderful! Just wait until you see Adam's

condo. It's incredible. And Houston has so much to see and do. I'm actually kind of jealous." Susan's ramble ended abruptly as she turned to Reed. "Once we're married, I want to go spend a weekend in Houston."

He took another bite of his sandwich and chewed, looking at her thoughtfully. Just when they all thought she'd burst if he kept her waiting any longer, he set the sandwich down, wiped his mouth with his napkin, and said, "Sure."

Susan reached over and slapped him on the arm. "That was mean, keeping me waiting like that."

"What? I had to think on it for a minute." Reed grinned, trying to act innocent and failing miserably.

"It's a good thing you're cute," she grumbled. Then she leaned over and kissed his cheek.

Garrett and Reed started talking about the weather and the traffic in Houston, and Susan commented about all the restaurants and coffee shops within walking distance of Adam's condo. Only Maggie remained quiet, eyes down, moving food around her plate with her fork.

"Miss Maggie, you okay?" Ashanti asked.

"I'm fine. But I'm gonna miss you." As she looked up, her eyes filled with tears and her lower lip started to tremble. Garrett placed his arm around her shoulders and pulled her to his chest.

"She's just goin' for a visit, Mags. She's been stuck here for three months. Let her go out and have some fun; see some new sights. She'll be back in no time with stories to tell from the big city."

Maggie swiped at her eyes and nodded. "I know, I know. It's just that things are changing, and I don't like it much. Ashanti's going to the city for a few days, I'm getting ready to go back to work and our cute little babies are growing up way too fast."

Ashanti felt her heart constrict. She knew she should tell Maggie she didn't intend to come back if she found a job. But she just couldn't bring herself to say anything.

****

The following week had passed in a blur. Maggie hadn't said anything to her about being in the way, and she was relieved. Susan hadn't been at the house as much and when she was there, she kept the wedding planning to a minimum, instead talking to Maggie and Ashanti about the kids in her class and how Reed was still stopping by on occasion to teach them new origami projects.

Friday night, Adam had arrived, and she'd been surprised how shy she felt around him. It was one thing to chat on the computer and another to see him in the flesh, knowing she'd be spending the next few days in his home, alone with him.

She almost backed out, but Maggie saw her apprehension and pulled her aside. "I can see you're having second thoughts, so I want to reassure you. I trust Adam and I know he'll be respectful and kind to you. But if you get there and start to feel uncomfortable for any reason, you call us, and we'll be there in a heartbeat to pick you up and bring you home."

For a moment, Ashanti wanted to confess she'd overheard her and Garrett, and knew they needed some time alone without her, but Jayla chose that moment to start crying. "Thank you, Miss Maggie. I 'preciate you lookin' out for me. "Scuse me."

She walked toward her room to get Jayla, and was startled when Adam walked out, Jayla in his arms. "I hope you don't mind, but I've been waiting for Miss Jayla here to wake up. When I heard her cry, I just had to go get her."

He looked so cute in his white outfit with his blond hair and her dark-skinned, natural-haired little baby in his arms, cooing and smiling, that she didn't mind at all. Seeing them together reminded her why she liked and trusted him. It was going to be okay; she knew it.

****

They were finally in Houston. The traffic had been insane, and Ashanti had plenty of time to gawk at all the people, traffic and buildings. She'd never been to such a big city and it was a shock going from a little farm to this bustling metropolis.

Adam kept looking over at her and grinning, as she turned this way and that, not wanting to miss a thing. "You remind me of me the first time I went to the county fair. I wanted to see everything, and I wanted time to slow down, so I didn't miss a thing."

"I never even 'magined a place could be so big. And there's so many people. And the buildings. I thought the barn was the biggest thing in the world and it's nothin' at all compared to this."

"Well, you've got time to take a good look 'round the next few days. For now, how 'bout we get you and Jayla settled into my guest room, then go get some dinner?"

"That sounds perfect, Adam, thank you. I've just

been sittin' this whole time while you drove, but I'm plum wore out."

"If you'd rather, we could order in, instead of going out to eat."

"Order in? You got a place that delivers here?"

Adam laughed. "We've got near enough every type of restaurant you could ever think of that delivers. There's Chinese, Thai, Sushi."

"Isn't sushi raw fish? I ain't interested in no raw fish. I don't even like fish when it's cooked. Unless it's deep fried. Then it's okay. But no way, no how am I eatin' raw fish."

"I wasn't suggestin' it, I was just saying." Adam laughed and shook his head as he pulled into an underground parking structure. "We can order whatever you *do* want to eat and nothin' you don't."

"Well alright, then, but what are we doin' down here?"

"This is where I live." At her look of disbelief, he added, "Not in the parking lot, of course. I live in the building up above."

"I ain't stupid, you know. I didn't 'spect you lived in the garage. But this building is fancy. You live in a fancy place?"

"Have you met me?" he asked, chuckling and

pulling into a reserved space. "Of course, I live in a fancy place."

She looked at him as he parked the car, her head tilted as she considered. "You're right. I should've known that."

He grinned then stepped out of the car, running around to open her door for her. Once she climbed out, he reached into the back seat to unbuckle the car seat and lift it out. He handed Jayla to her mom, grabbed the luggage from the trunk, then led the way to the elevator.

When the doors opened, Ashanti gasped. The interior of the elevator was decorated with mirrors and wood paneling, with a plush carpet floor. But that wasn't what surprised her the most. Inside was a small man in a red and gold uniform with tassels. As she gaped at him, he stepped forward.

"Hello, Mr. Donahue, so nice to see you. Let me take that for you." He grabbed the luggage and placed it in the back of the elevator while Adam took the car seat from Ashanti and gestured for her to enter. Once they were all aboard, the man pushed a button and turned to Adam.

"Who do we have here?" he asked, looking at the sleeping baby.

"This is my friend Ms. Jones and her daughter,

Jayla. They'll be staying with me for a few days and checking out the big city. Ashanti, this is Mr. Cahill. He's the best elevator attendant this side of the Mississippi."

"I don't know about that but I'm one of the few attendants left, anyway. Oh, she's so precious." The man fussed over the baby, then held out his hand to Ashanti. "It's so very nice to meet you, Ms. Jones. Please let me know if there's anything I can do for you. Anything at all."

She didn't know what to say, so she shook his hand and tried to keep from staring at him. Adam smirked at her and she made a face back at him.

When they reached Adam's floor, number 19, the elevator doors slid open with a whisper and revealed a long hallway lined with deep gray carpet with a swirl design. The walls were a rich cream color and the doors were made from a dark, textured wood with ornate handles.

Ashanti followed Adam and Mr. Cahill down the hallway to a double door with a large "D" on it. There was a discreet plaque stating the apartment number, 1920. The attendant set the bags down and shook hands with Adam, then trotted back to the elevator.

She was shocked when Adam chucked her under her chin. "What? Why'd you do that?"

"I felt like I needed to shove your eyes back in your head, but I settled for closing your gaping jaw."

"I don't have no gaping jaw and my eyes are just fine, thank you very much."

"Don't get het up; I'm just teasing you. I remember the first time I saw this place. I had the same reaction. It's quite...something."

"Something ain't even close," she muttered, and he let out a bark of laughter.

He unlocked his door and pushed it open, stepping back to let her enter first. After the elevator, the attendant and the hallway, what she saw took her breath away.

"Oh, Adam! I don't believe it!" She walked into the apartment, looking around in wonder. The interior was decorated in a style similar to the farmhouse. Wainscoting on the walls and wooden plank flooring. A large stone fireplace in the middle of the room. A dark brown leather sofa and chair that looked like they were twins to Garrett's filled a small, sunken living room off to the side. The kitchen was the only thing that was modern looking, sporting stainless steel appliances, an island with a marble countertop, and a small breakfast nook tucked in the corner.

As she turned around, feeling more at home than she'd expected, she noticed the photos that hung all around the apartment. There were pictures of the farmhouse, a ranch, Adam's family, and scenes from the city. Even though she didn't know much about art, she knew the photos were really good, and she knew they'd been taken by the same photographer.

"These are yours, aren't they?" she asked.

Adam shrugged and nodded. "Yeah. I like taking pictures of things. It's pretty cool to capture an instant in time and be able to recall it whenever you want."

"They're really 'mazing, Adam." He shrugged again and ducked his head. She realized she'd embarrassed him and that wasn't the best way to start her visit, so she asked, "Hey, can I see my room?"

He grinned at her and led her off to the left, to the end of a short hallway. "This here's the guest room." He pushed the door open with his knee and this time her jaw dropped to the ground. "I thought you might like it."

She walked in and touched the quilt on the bed.

It was a bold design, like her favorite muumuu and skirts. There were splashes of color everywhere, but they were classy, not gaudy. The bed was a four-poster bed, with tall, white spindles. There was a dresser and a nightstand in the same crisp white, with handles made from colored glass that reflected the late afternoon sun. The window was huge, and she had an amazing view of the city.

She turned back to thank him, but he was placing Jayla into a small crib on the other side of the bed. It was white, too, with bedding covered with farm animals. Adam turned and saw her watching him. "I hope you don't mind. When I saw the sheets, I had to get them. I thought she might miss the animals at Stony Gulch, and these would make her feel less homesick."

Ashanti had a sudden urge to throw her arms around him and hug him. He looked so cute, standing there next to her daughter, but she knew she shouldn't. The awkward moment ended with Adam gesturing to the door behind her.

"You have your own bathroom right back there. It only has a shower, so I bought a baby tub for Jayla to use. It fits into the bathtub in my room, so feel free to use it when she needs a bath."

The thought of being in his bathroom made her

feel all uncomfortable inside, so she walked into hers and took a look, hoping to compose herself. It was beautiful. The walls were a deep teal with gold fixtures and a gold, raised sink in the vanity. The shower had white tiles with streaks of gold and teal running through them and a large, gold-plated shower head. There were plush towels tucked into an open cabinet and a multi-colored terry robe hung on the back of the door. She lifted the robe and walked out towards Adam with one eyebrow raised.

"It seemed more your style than a plain, white robe," he offered.

She couldn't help it, she had to hug him. She walked over and placed her arms around him. "Thank you for making me feel like I matter," she whispered. As she let go and moved back, she saw his stricken expression.

"Of course, you matter," he said. "Why on earth would you say that?"

Tears filled her eyes and she shook her head. "I don't know. It's been a long day is all. I'm plum wore out." He didn't seem to be buying it, so she added. "I still got all them mommy hormones racin' through me, so there's that." This time he nodded, apparently satisfied with her answer.

"How 'bout I leave you alone for a bit and let you

get settled. You can meet me out at the kitchen in 30 minutes and we can decide what we want to do for dinner. How does that sound?"

"It sounds wonderful, thank you."

"Okay then, I'll see you in a bit." As he walked towards the door he looked back over his shoulder. "If there's anything I forgot or anything you need, you just let me know, okay?"

Tears filled her eyes again and she couldn't get any words out, so she just nodded. *So, this is what it feels like to be cherished*, she thought. *I could get used to this.*

4

Ashanti wiped the dribble of formula from Jayla's chin. "You a messy baby, you know that?" Jayla responded with a smile and she grinned at her daughter. "You sure are a sweet thing. Even if you're messy."

She set the bottle on the coffee table and shifted so she could lay Jayla on her lap. "What should we do today? Adam went to work and we're on our own for the first time, ever."

She looked around the apartment and tried to decide what to do. She wasn't used to having time on her hands. At the farm, she'd been busy taking care of Jayla and Walker or talking with Maggie or Susan. She'd learned to gather eggs from the henhouse and throw feed for the chickens. She hadn't been willing to milk a cow or go near the goats, but Maggie assured her she was making progress.

Here, she felt out of her element, in more ways than one. She wasn't used to being in a big city and this condo was extremely fancy. She wasn't used to nice things and it was a little overwhelming. She was glad that the inside was more like home, though. Adam had done a good job of that. She'd expected everything to be white, with glass and chrome; not homey and warm, like this. Adam was quite the mystery.

When she and Jayla got up this morning, they'd wandered out to the kitchen where there was heavenly smelling coffee. Adam was standing with his back to her and when he turned, she was speechless for a full minute. He was wearing a dark gray suit and tie with a white shirt, black, shiny boots, and a dark gray Stetson.

"What? Do I have lettuce in my teeth or something?"

"You aren't wearing white. Or rhinestones. Who are you and what did you do with Adam?"

He laughed. "I'm head of the research and development department of a large agricultural company. I'm expected to dress a certain way, so I do. I like my job and want to keep it, so I make some concessions." He straightened his tie and grinned at her. "But underneath, I'm wearing boxers that say, 'Bite Me' in gold glitter. He winked at her and she let out a belly laugh.

"You've got my number. Just text me or call if you need anything. I'm sorry I got called into work today. I was hoping to take today off to show you around."

"No worries. Me and Jayla got this. I'm still tired so we'll probably just hang around here for a bit, then maybe go for a walk or something."

"Oh! That reminds me." He walked over to a closet near the front door and opened it. "I got you and Jayla a present." He rolled out a *very* nice stroller.

She looked up at Adam. "Is there anythin' you didn't buy for my daughter?"

His cheeks turned pink, and he shrugged. "What can I say. I like her and I had fun getting these things. So, sue me."

He grabbed a set of keys from the side table. "Remember, there's a set of keys for you right here. But if you forget, you can always ask Mr. Cahill to let you in."

He kissed Jayla on her cheek, waved goodbye to

Ashanti and ducked out the door, leaving her wishing for a quick kiss on her own cheek.

****

She and Jayla had spent the morning exploring the apartment and now that lunch was done, they were ready to try out the stroller and take a walk. It had taken a while to figure out the stroller, but with Mr. Cahill's help, she'd been able to get Jayla strapped in and ready to go.

The streets of downtown Houston were bustling, and the sidewalk was crowded, but Ashanti found that she enjoyed the noise and the energy. She'd always lived in small towns and it was exciting to be here. She walked until her legs and feet started to ache, then she turned around and headed back.

They'd finally arrived at Adam's building and she leaned against the wall while she waited for the elevator. Jayla had slept most of the time, but when she'd been awake, she'd seemed as enthralled as Ashanti. It was a whole different world here, and she was grateful her daughter didn't seem to mind.

She straightened up as the elevator arrived, groaning as her muscles complained at the movement. The doors opened and Mr. Cahill grinned with delight. He stepped aside to let her in and pushed the stroller in behind her.

"How was your walk, Ms. Jones and little Miss Jones?"

"It was lovely, Mr. Cahill, but mama's dogs are barkin', if you know what I mean."

He laughed and pushed the button to take them to Floor Nineteen. "I sure do, Ms. Jones. When I first started working here, my legs would be so tired at the end of my shift. After a while, though, I got used to being on my feet all day. Now it feels strange to sit."

"Well, I ain't never gonna get to a point where I prefer standing to sittin'. No sir!"

Mr. Cahill laughed. "You were gone awhile, so you must have gotten the hang of the stroller. It's one of the nicest I've ever seen. Mr. Donahue sure has good taste."

"Yep; it almost drives itself. I wondered if I could just let go and it would lead us home." She chuckled, then sighed. "I really do 'preciate you helpin' me figure it out. I've never seen a stroller like this. The fanciest one I ever saw before this was an umbrella stroller with a flip down hood to keep the sun off the baby."

They arrived at her floor and Mr. Cahill helped

her navigate out. "I was happy to help, Ms. Jones. I enjoyed fiddlin' with this contraption. It made my day."

She waved goodbye to him as the doors closed and the elevator took off. She pushed Jayla towards the apartment door, ready to get something cool to drink and put her feet up for a spell. As she was pulling the keys out of her purse, she heard a muffled bark. She turned and looked down the hall, but there was nothing there. She shrugged and unlocked the door. She pushed the stroller in and turned to shut the door, but a flash of white caught her eye.

"What the heck?" She looked back at her daughter, asleep in the stroller. She was curious about the bark and all, but she needed to get Jayla into her bed. She took one last look down the empty hallway, then shut the door.

She unstrapped Jayla and lifted her from the stroller. Her daughter smelled of baby and sunshine and she buried her face in her neck. How she loved this little child. She'd never regret any of the things that led up to this moment. She liked who she'd become, and she adored her daughter. *Life is good*, she thought. She placed the baby in the crib, covered her with a light blanket and headed for the kitchen to get a glass of iced tea, with lots of ice cubes.

As she set the glass down on the coffee table and prepared to sit, she thought she heard a noise at the door. She froze for a second, listening. Sure enough, there was a snuffling noise. She walked over to the door and looked out the peephole. Nothing. She shrugged and started to walk away, but she heard it again, along with a whimper. Ashanti threw the door open. There on the doorstep was a fluffy white dog. His tongue was hanging out, sideways and she couldn't help but laugh.

"Well, hello there, little doggie. Where did you come from?" she asked. She leaned down and checked the tag on his collar. "Wylie, huh. Nice to meet you, Wylie." As she stood back up, the dog ran past her into the apartment.

"Oh no you don't. You may be cute and all, but this ain't no home for wayward doggies. You gotta go." He'd hopped up on the table and was lapping up her iced tea with gusto. "Really dog? You had to go and ruin my drink? I'm gonna have to burn that glass now, you know. Or at the very least, sterilize it so I don't get no doggy cooties or nothin'."

Wylie was still drinking but she pulled the glass away from him. He whined and shook his head, leaving drops of tea all over the table. "Now look what you did," she said, shaking her own head. She walked to the kitchen and pulled a plastic container from the garbage. It was from their dinner the night before and should be fine for a temporary water bowl. She rinsed it out and filled it with fresh, cold tap water.

Wylie was dancing around her legs and when she set the bowl on the floor, he nearly toppled it in his haste to drink. Ashanti pulled another glass from the cupboard and poured a fresh iced tea for herself, then sat on the sofa. Having satisfied his thirst, Wylie ran over and jumped up next to her.

"Oh no you don't. You ain't allowed on this here sofa, no matter how cute you may be," she said sternly. As she reached to push him onto the floor, he held a paw up in the air in front of her. She felt her breath catch in her throat.

"What on earth?" she grabbed his paw and lifted it, to take a better look. The bottom of Wylie's paw was covered in a red substance. She lifted his other paws, and all four were stained red.

Her heart started pounding and she pulled him onto her lap. She checked him to see if he'd been hurt, but the only sign something was wrong was the red on his feet. She checked his tag again, but it only said his name; there was no address or phone number.

Wylie curled up in her lap, let out a big sigh, and fell asleep, leaving Ashanti to wonder what she'd gotten herself into this time.

5

While Jayla and Wylie slept, Ashanti had time to put her feet up, drink her iced tea and think. Her first instinct had been to call Adam. Maybe he knew who this dog belonged to. Maybe its owner was an artist, and this was just red paint. Maybe . . .no, who was she kidding. She knew blood when she saw it. This dog had blood on his feet, no doubt about it.

She decided to check with Mr. Cahill, as soon as Jayla woke up. She wasn't about to wake her baby for what might be nothing more than a runaway dog. She'd just be patient, sip her tea and rest, with a bloody-footed, furry white dog on her lap. Ashanti chuckled. She'd never liked dogs, and they hadn't been partial to her either. But this dog seemed to have taken a shine to her, and even though she'd never admit it, he was pretty cute.

The sound of Jayla moving around in the guestroom woke Wylie, who stretched, yawned and ran off to investigate the sounds. Ashanti followed him and found her daughter giggling, her hand stuck through the slats of the crib while Wylie licked it.

"All right you two cuties. I'm gonna feed this pretty little lady, change her diaper and then we're goin' 'vestigatin'. We need to find out where you came from and what that is all over your paws.

She lifted Jayla out of the crib and kissed her cheek, causing her to squeal with delight, while Wylie ran around her legs, his tongue lolling out the side of his mouth.

****

She'd fed Jayla and changed her, given Wylie some fresh water and a slice of bologna Adam had in the fridge, and now they were ready to look for Wylie's home. Ashanti pushed the stroller out the front door and once Wylie had joined her, she shut and locked it.

"All right doggie. Be like Lassie and lead the

way." She waited, but Wylie just sat there, looking at her with his head cocked to the side. She sighed.

"Of course, it ain't never that easy. Fine then. We'll go find Mr. Cahill. I'm bettin' he knows who you belong to."

The three of them headed to the elevator and pushed the call button. While she waited, she glanced up and down the hallway, looking for any clues. Just before the elevator arrived, she noticed a faint trail of small red paw prints in the hallway.

She looked up as the elevator doors slid open, ready to ask the attendant if he knew Wylie, but there was nobody there.

"Hmm. Maybe he's takin' a break or somethin'. Elevator attendants gotta pee, too."

Suddenly, Wylie growled. She looked down and he was standing with his tail straight up, his teeth bared, a snarl on his doggie lips.

"What is it boy," she whispered. He backed up, pressing against her legs, and she felt the hair stand up on the back of her neck. "Come on, we need to get out of here." Ashanti turned and pushed the stroller quickly down the hallway, back to Adam's. Her hands shook as she pulled the keys out and unlocked the door. She looked back down the hallway several times but didn't see anyone or anything.

Wylie kept growling, staying between them and whatever threat he was sensing. Finally, she got the door open and shoved the stroller inside. Wylie ran in and positioned himself next to Jayla, who was blissfully unaware of the tension.

She closed the door quickly and quietly, her heart racing as she looked out the peephole. Still nobody there. She breathed a sigh of relief and pushed the stroller into the guest room. She was about to unbuckle Jayla when Wylie suddenly stopped growling and stood stock still, eyes glued to the front door.

Ashanti pulled the guest room door closed, shutting her daughter and Wylie inside. She crept over to the entryway, placing her back flat against the wall next to the door. She stood still, listening, for several seconds. When she didn't hear anything, she cautiously looked out the peephole.

In the hallway, facing away from her, was a tall man. He was dressed in jeans and a dark blue sweatshirt, with black shoes and brown hair. He was squatted down, looking at the floor, and as she watched, he leaned down further and ran his hand over one of Wylie's paw prints.

Oh dang! She'd seen the prints earlier when she'd been waiting for the elevator. They led straight to Adam's apartment. As if he heard her thoughts, the man stood up and turned, facing her. She stepped back and placed her back against the wall again, her heart pounding furiously.

As she held her breath, listening for any sound from the man, she saw the handle of the door turn and she had to shove her hand in her mouth to keep from screaming. Luckily, she'd locked and deadbolted the door when they'd come in, so even though the knob turned a bit, the door didn't open.

Ashanti heard a grunt of frustration and then it sounded like the man knelt down and looked under the door. She was grateful she'd moved to the side, where he couldn't see her feet, but she was shaking so bad she was sure he could feel the vibration through the wall.

"Hey, it's me. I can't find the stupid dog. I think he might have gone into another apartment, but nobody's home." She held her breath as she listened to the man's voice, apparently talking to someone on the phone. "All right. Other than the dog, we're all done here. I'll see you in a few." The doorknob twisted once again before she heard the man walk away. She heard the ding of the elevator arriving, and the sound of the doors swishing closed. She waited a few more seconds before she risked a look through the peephole. The hallway was clear.

Ashanti made it to the bedroom, closed the door behind her, and lifted Jayla out of the stroller before her legs gave way. She slid to the floor and sat there, hugging Jayla tightly, while Wylie climbed onto her lap and curled up next to the baby.

She looked down into his chocolate brown eyes. "Thank you for staying with Jayla and thank you both for bein' quiet. Right now, I gotta rest for a minute, then I gotta think. Somethin's going on, somethin' bad if my gut's right, and you, cute doggie, got us all caught up in the middle of it."

6

*A*shanti looked out the peephole, one last time, then opened the door and looked both ways. Nobody was in the hallway, so she pushed the stroller out of the apartment, shut the door and made sure it was locked, then hustled to the elevator. By the time it arrived, she was panting heavily, and her underarms were drenched with sweat.

Mr. Cahill glanced at her as she pushed the stroller in, not even waiting for a greeting. "Why Ms. Jones, is everything all right?" he asked.

"No, not really," she admitted. She leaned down and lifted the blanket off the stroller. "You wouldn't happen to recognize this little fella?" Under the blanket, Jayla and Wylie were snuggled up, both fast asleep.

"Why, I think I do, Ms. Jones. That's Wylie. He belongs to the gentleman in Apartment 1905." He frowned. "It's odd that he's here, though. Mr. Bedford isn't due back for another week."

"What apartment did you mention? And what's the dead man's name?" Ashanti asked.

"Apartment 1905," he paused. "Excuse me, Ms. Jones. Did you say, 'dead man's name'?"

"I sure did, Mr. Cahill. I sure did." The sweat dripped down her back and she shifted to pull the fabric away from her skin. "I thought this was gonna be a relaxin' vacation. But no, no sir, it ain't. I don't know for sure what's goin' on, but it's somethin' bad, fo sure. Mmhmm."

The elevator attendant was still confused, and he looked at her, his mouth hanging slightly open, his eyes wide. "Why do you say Mr. Bedford is dead?"

"Because this here doggie had blood all over his paws. And a big, scary dude was trying to find him. I don't know how, but we got ourselves a mystery and I think it's a murder mystery, all right."

Mr. Cahill was still staring at her, but she could see the wheels turning. "Tell me from the beginning, then we can call Mr. Donahue and the authorities, if need be."

****

"Why didn't you call me right away?" Adam's voice condemned her through the phone.

"I was going to, but Jayla was asleep, and I didn't want to worry you. I thought it was no big deal until that man checked out our door." As Adam's silence dragged on, she realized what she'd said. "I mean, checked out *your* door."

He sighed and she could practically see him run his hands through his hair. "I understand. If you'd called me right away, I probably would've told you not to worry. But now, I'm worried enough for both of us."

Strangely enough, his words made her heart beat faster and her face felt warm. She looked up and Mr. Cahill was grinning at her. She made a face at him and when Adam asked her to put the attendant on the phone, she handed it over.

"Yes, Mr. Donahue. Certainly, sir. I'll make sure they're taken care of till you get here." He hung up the phone and stuffed it into his pocket. "Well, ladies, and Wylie, you're going to get a real treat. I'm taking you up to the penthouse suite on the top floor." He grinned and pulled a tiny key out of another pocket. He slid it into a tiny keyhole in the wall panel, twisted it, and the elevator took off.

"What about the owner. Won't they be upset to find a woman, a child and a dog in their home?" she asked.

He shook his head. "No ma'am. The penthouse is reserved for special guests, or emergency situations. It doesn't belong to any one person."

Jayla chose that moment to yawn and stretch, capturing their attention and defusing the tension.

"She sure is a cutie," Mr. Cahill said.

"I think so, but I'm a lil' bit prejudiced." Ashanti laughed, reaching down to stroke her daughter's cheek.

"Mr. Donahue seems pretty taken with her," he continued. "Matter of fact, he seems pretty taken with you, too."

She turned and faced him, hands on her hips. "You tryin' to start somethin', Mr. Cahill? Cause I think you tryin' to start somethin'."

He laughed and shook his head. "No, ma'am, just making conversation."

She squinted her eyes at him. "Mmhm."

The elevator arrived and the doors opened. Her

breath caught in her throat as she took in the penthouse suite. "Wow! I ain't never seen nothin' like this in my life."

"Most people haven't. It's pretty--special."

She moved forward as he steered the stroller out of the elevator. "The kitchen's right through there and it's fully stocked. You're free to use anything you want. I have to get back to attending, but I'll check in on you and let you know when Mr. Donahue arrives." He paused and his face got serious. "I'm the only one with a key to this place. I promise, you'll be safe here."

Ashanti stood staring after him as he walked into the elevator and pushed a button. The doors swished closed and he was gone. A small coo sounded from the stroller and she looked down. Wylie and Jayla were looking up at her, expectantly.

"What, y'all. You thirsty or somethin'?" She reached down and released the straps, then picked up her daughter. Wylie jumped to the ground and furiously shook out his fur. "I sure hope I don't have to vacuum up all that doggie hair," she grumbled. His tail wagged and his tongue lolled to the side of his mouth as he watched her. "Fine, then. Let's go check out the grub in this dump. I crack myself up," she chuckled to herself as she led the way to the kitchen.

****

"Thank you so much, Mr. Cahill, I really 'preciate you takin' care of them till I could get here," Adam's voice roused Ashanti and she tried to sit up on the couch where she'd fallen asleep. She was pinned in place by a weight across her chest and one across her legs.

"What is this?" His delight at her predicament annoyed her.

"Help me up, Adam and quit gawking."

"Why, it's not every day that I get to see you all disheveled and mussed up," he teased. "I wanna take a long look."

"You do that, and it'll be the last thing you ever see." Her voice sounded sweet, but the venom in her eyes had him hustling to lift Jayla off her chest and shoo the dog from her legs. He bounced the baby in his arms and placed a kiss on her cheek, making her squeal with delight.

"How's my girl?" he cooed back.

Wylie was watching him closely. He seemed to

be wondering if he should trust him or bite him, and Ashanti laughed out loud.

"What's so funny?"

"You may have Jayla wrapped around your finger, but Wylie here isn't so easy to win over," she told him.

"Really? I'll have to work on that. But how about Jayla's mama? How does she feel about me?" He looked her in the eye and her heart started to race faster.

"Well, I'm glad you're here. I'm not quite sure what's going on and it's a little hard to navigate a murder 'vestigation while tryin' to wrangle a dog and a daughter."

He looked disappointed by her answer and her heart constricted. She didn't want to hurt his feelings, but she didn't want to lead him on, either. She knew he cared about her, and she cared back, but she had some things to figure out before she made any decisions.

"I was thinkin' bout this on the drive over, and I think you and Jayla should head back to Stony Gulch."

"You're pullin' my leg? Right? You best be pullin' my leg." Ashanti was angry; how dare he tell her she should skedaddle back to safety. She was a grown woman for Pete's sake. As she glared at him, she caught the movement at the corner of his mouth and instantly calmed down. "You ARE pulling my leg."

"Well, yeah; I have met you," he grinned.

"That's not funny and it's not a very nice thing to do, Adam. I've already had a stressful day. You're supposed to be supportive and kind, not a . . . jerk!" She ruined her tirade by grinning back at him, and they both chuckled.

"The way I see it, we need to check out this doggie's home. Mr. Cahill told me his apartment number, and I say we go take a look."

"I agree, but how we gonna get in, if the door's locked?"

Adam grinned and reached into his back pocket. He pulled out his wallet, then a thin, black case. He opened it and she saw tiny lock picking tools in his hand.

"No way! You know how to pick a lock?"

"Of course," he told her. "Out on the farm, if you forgot your key, you usually didn't have time to ride all the way back to the house to get it. Lots of times my brothers lost the key in the pasture or some such and my dad told us the next time he had to replace a lock we broke because we lost the key, he was gonna whoop us all. So, I learned to pick the locks and save the day." He stuck the tools back in their case, then back in his pocket.

"Sometimes you really amaze me," she said softly.

"Only sometimes? I guess I'd better try harder." Adam waggled his eyebrows at her, and she shook her head at him.

"Enough, Adam Donahue. We've got some serious business to handle."

"You're right," he conceded. "How about I put Jayla and the dog in the stroller while you make a list of things you need from my apartment."

"Why would I do that?"

"Because Mr. Cahill was kind enough to get permission for us to stay here for a couple of days." When she started to protest, he raised his hands in the air. "I know, you don't want to, and you can take care of yourself. But truth is, we don't know what's goin' on. It could be nothin' or it could be something. Until we know more, I think we should stay here, for good measure."

She knew he was right, but she really liked his apartment. She told him so, then while he got the stroller ready, she made a list.

"Okay, we're ready when you are."

They proceeded to the elevator doors. "How are

we gonna get out of here," Ashanti asked. Adam held up the tiny key Mr. Cahill had given him. They rode the elevator to Adam's floor, and exited. Ashanti led the way to his apartment, and they hurried in, locking the door behind them.

She was sweating again, her nerves on fire. She wondered how Maggie and Reed always looked so calm and cool when they were sleuthing. She looked over at Adam who was pulling a couple of duffle bags out of the closet. Wylie and Jayla were cuddling in the stroller, the baby's arm resting on the dog's back.

"Here you go." Adam handed her a bag. "You can use this for Jayla's stuff. I'm going to start in the bathroom and collect toiletries and such. There's food for us upstairs, but I want to grab a few supplies from the kitchen, too. He pushed the stroller to the bedroom door, then hurried off.

Ashanti sighed. She packed her stuff and Jayla's, then made sure she got the bowl of water and food she'd set down for the dog. She was checking her list to see if she'd missed anything when she heard Wylie growl.

He was standing, facing the door, with his tail standing up straight. Adam appeared and quickly pushed the stroller into the bedroom. The dog went with Jayla and once they were inside, he pulled the door shut. He motioned for her to follow him and they tiptoed towards the door.

Ashanti stood to the side, again, with her back against the wall, while he peered out the peephole. She saw his eyes go wide and he slid up next to her. She felt his arm brush hers and she grabbed his hand, holding on tightly.

"Still nobody here, boss. I'm tellin' you, the dog must've run away. I know the pawprints lead to this door, but it's dead quiet. Don't look like nobody's been here all day."

She squeezed Adam's hand tighter, and he squeezed back. They heard the man walk away, his keys jangling from the chain hanging from his pocket.

7

"Do you have everything you need?" Adam's whisper was strained, and Ashanti looked up into his face. His cheeks were flushed and his eyes wide. His lips were drawn tight and she could feel the tension radiating off of him.

"Adam?"

He sighed and tried to relax his shoulders. "I want you and Jayla out of here right now. We're staying upstairs until this whole mess is over." He grimaced and took a deep breath. He blew it out and looked at her upturned face. "It's okay, Ashanti. I ain't angry. It's just. . . if anything happened to you, I don't know what I'd do."

His admission touched her heart, and she

reached up to stroke his cheek. "Then let's get the heck out of here."

He grabbed her hand and kissed her palm. "You grab the stroller and I'll grab all the bags."

"Deal!" she said, smirking at him like she'd won something.

She pushed the stroller to the door while he slung the duffle bags' straps over his shoulders. When they were ready, he checked the hallway. "All clear." They hustled to the elevator. She didn't even realize she'd been holding her breath until the doors closed, Adam inserted the key, and they were on their way up to the penthouse. It looked much more accommodating this time around, and she pushed the stroller to the guest room, with two beds.

"I thought you'd want the master bedroom," Adam said, surprised by her actions.

"Nope. I want the bedroom where we can both have our own beds but still be near each other." Her matter-of-fact tone didn't quite hide her nerves, but he just looked at her, wisely not saying anything. He shrugged and followed her lead.

Her heart was pounding in her chest. She'd been scared the first time the man was at the door, but this second time had taken the wind out of her sails. She was terrified. She wanted to hold Jayla in her arms and have Adam wrap his around both of them, to keep them safe. She wanted to curl up in bed, pull the covers over her head and stay like that until the world was right again. She wanted...

Adam was watching her, a stricken expression on his face. She could see he was worried about her, and that made her feel bad. "What you lookin' at me like that for?" She put her hand on her hip and glared at him.

Confused, he just looked at her. "I'm trying to figure out what's goin' on in that mind of yours."

"Well, I'm thinkin' I want a nice cold cola with lots of ice. Then I want to feed Jayla and Wylie. Then you and me and them are gonna go do some 'vestigatin'."

Adam walked closer and leaned down, his face only inches from hers. "You know it makes me crazy when you talk all tough like that," he whispered. He kissed her nose and before she knew it, he was gone.

She felt her face flame and her palms go sweaty. *Get a grip, girl*, she told herself. She caught sight of herself in the mirror and saw the silly grin on her face. She changed her expression to a stern one and told herself, *this ain't the time nor place for those kinds of thoughts.*

"Your cold drink is ready," he called.

"Okay, we'll be there in a minute." She lifted her daughter from the stroller and carried her to the living room, Wylie following at her heels. She sat down on the sofa and picked up her drink from the coffee table. "Mmm, that hits the spot."

Wylie walked over to Adam, who sat in an armchair across from Ashanti. He stopped in front of him, sat and looked up, his head tilted to the side.

"What?" Adam asked. "I got broccoli in my teeth or somethin'?"

The little dog apparently decided he was all right, because he jumped up onto Adam's lap. "Whoa, there. I didn't say you could do that." He laughed as Wylie licked at his face, then snuggled up next to him on the chair. "I guess he likes me."

"I'd say so," she replied. The microwave dinged and she looked up at him.

"I took the liberty of warmin' up a bottle for Jayla. I hope you don't mind."

She scowled at him. "Course I mind. I hate it when you try to take care of my daughter." She stood up and handed the baby to him. "Here, hold her for a minute."

She went into the kitchen and pulled the bottle from the microwave. As she walked out of the kitchen, she realized Wylie's bowl was still packed.

She handed the bottle to Adam and went into the bedroom. She pulled the bowl out and filled it with water. She set it on the floor in the kitchen, then looked around. Surely there was something she could feed Wylie.

"Mr. Cahill said there's pet food in the pantry."

"How did you know what I was . . .oh, never mind. Thanks." She found a can of dog food, opened it and jumped when the dog ran into the room. "You scared me, Wylie!" she laughed, setting the food on the floor. He lapped at it, then drank some water, then went back to the food.

She left him to it and returned to the living room. Jayla was happily drinking her bottle, safe in Adam's arms.

****

Jayla was asleep in the stroller and Wylie had finished his food. "I think he's gonna need a potty break, soon," Ashanti declared.

"I was talking with Mr. Cahill about that and he said Mr. Bedford has a special set up in his apartment for those times when he's not home. He called it his 'pee pad,' and he said it's a square of plastic 'grass' that doesn't leak and is easy to clean.

He told me we can take it, if we happen to get access to it."

"But what if the apartment's a crime scene, Adam? We can't go takin' stuff from a crime scene. I think that's a crime in itself."

He looked thoughtful for a moment, then nodded. "Let's take it one step at a time. First, we gotta find the place and see if we can get in. Then we can check it out. If it 'pears to be a crime scene, we'll back out, slowly and come back here. Once you and Jayla are settled, I'll take the danged dog for a walk."

"Don't call him a 'danged dog.' He's kinda cute, once you get over all the shedding and licking and stuff."

"Why Ashanti Jones, I do believe you have a heart, after all!"

"What? Why would you say that to me, course I got a heart."

"Those goats back at the farm didn't get no love from you, if I recall."

She shrugged her shoulders. "Well they smelled bad, and they were creepy. Wylie here is cute and soft and he took to Jayla like . . .I don't know, but you get my drift."

Adam laughed softly. "Yes ma'am, I do." He

sighed and rubbed his hand down his face. "You ready to do this?"

"Ready as I'll ever be," she replied. They pushed the stroller to the door, paused for the dog to hop in, then Adam covered the dog and baby with a light blanket. He inserted the key and called the elevator while Ashanti stood still, hands on the stroller handle.

The elevator arrived and she pushed the stroller in, turned and Adam pushed the down button. When they arrived at the 19th floor, he stood in the elevator doorway, fists clenched, ready to protect them if need be. The doors slid open and he looked up and down the hallway.

"All clear," he whispered. He motioned for her to push the stroller out as he kept watch.

"Which way do we go?" she asked.

"Mr. Cahill said it was this way." He started walking to the left and she followed him closely, looking back over her shoulder every so often. Adam stopped in front of apartment 1905, looked both ways, then casually pulled the lock picking tools from his pocket. Ashanti turned the stroller away from the door and leaned over to check on her two "babies." Jayla was sound asleep, her thumb resting on her lips, as if she'd just stopped sucking it. Wylie was alert, his ears standing up and his eyes bright.

"Take it easy, doggie," she whispered. "Don't cause a fuss now." As if he understood, he rested his chin on his paws and looked up at her, his big doggie eyes making her chuckle.

"Got it!" Adam pushed the door open, slowly, then looked at Ashanti. "Wait here for a moment, while I take a look. Anybody comes near you, you scream, and I'll be right here to save you."

"Save me? Excuse me, did you just say you'd save me?" She tried to sound angry, but mostly she was worried. She was certain that was why he'd tried to rile her up, so she played along. Adam winked at her and went inside the apartment. It seemed like forever before he reappeared, but it was probably only a couple of minutes. He waved her in and shut the door behind them.

"It doesn't look like this is a crime scene. If it is, they did a dang good job of cleaning it up." He pushed the stroller to the side of the doorway, then lifted the blanket. Wylie hopped out and ran for the back of the apartment. The two of them followed and watched as he sniffed around what was apparently the master bedroom. He stopped under the window and looked up, then he scratched at the wall, whining softly, and turned to look at them.

Adam walked over and looked out the window. He bent to pet Wylie on the head. He unlatched the window and leaned out. When he stood up again, he had a square of artificial grass in his hands. He set it on the floor and Wylie immediately walked over and relieved himself on it.

"Gross!" Ashanti declared. Adam laughed.

He walked around the room, looking thoughtful. "Is it just me, or is something missing?"

She retraced his steps, ending up just behind him. "I don't know what you see that I don't."

"It's not what I see so much as what I don't see," he said, cryptically. She shook her head and he explained. "Look at the living room and the dining room floors."

She looked. She turned around and looked at the bedroom floor. She bent down and took a closer look. The hardwood floor was beautiful, but the center of the floor was decidedly darker than the rest of the floor. Her eyes grew big as she realized what that meant. "There used to be a rug here," she whispered. She looked back at the Persian carpets on the floor of the living room and the dining room.

"Yep. I think this is our crime scene, and they

removed the rug to hide the evidence." Adam's voice sounded strained and she looked up at him. "I didn't want to believe anything bad had happened, but it's lookin' like it did."

She nodded and looked over at Wylie, sitting on the floor next to the bed with a sad look on his little doggie face.

****

Adam finished taking pictures of the scene with his cell phone, took a trash bag from a box on the counter and stuck Wylie's pee pad inside.

"Yuck!" Ashanti wrinkled her nose at him.

"What?" We need to call the police and tell them we found Wylie. If they find out we entered this apartment illegally, we'll be in trouble. They can't find fresh pee in here, you know. And I don't want to take the time to wash it off. This place gives me the willies. Let's just get out of here and I'll take care of it upstairs."

She knew he was right, but it still kind of grossed her out, so she just shrugged. "Good thing I'm pushin' the stroller and you got your hands free, cause I ain't carryin' that--no way, no how."

Adam grinned. "You're so cute when you're complaining."

She made a face at him, called Wylie, and once he'd jumped up and settled in the stroller next to Jayla, she pushed the stroller towards the door.

Adam tucked the garbage bag under his arm. He looked out the peephole, then slowly opened the door. "All clear."

She'd pushed the stroller into the hallway and was headed for the elevator when she heard it start up. "Oh no, oh no, oh no." She turned to Adam who was standing still, an odd look on his face.

"Come on, let's go to my apartment, hurry!"

He raced over to the door and pulled out his keys, dropping the garbage bag in the process. Ashanti was right behind him when the elevator dinged, signaling it was stopping on their floor. Adam pushed the door open and shoved the stroller inside. His eyes widened when he saw the garbage bag on the ground next to Ashanti. The elevator doors started to open, and in a panic, she reached down, grabbed the bag, and the two of them fell through the door, shutting it behind them.

They could hear someone talking to Mr. Cahill, then the elevator left. They heard a door down the hallway open and close, then there was silence.

Ashanti looked up at Adam and noticed his mouth was twitching.

"What's wrong with you?" she whispered. "You havin' a stroke or something?"

He chuckled. "Look down."

She did and realized she was still holding the bag with the pee pad. "Oh gross!" she exclaimed, dropping it on the floor. It made a squishy "plop" and she shuddered. "Don't you dare laugh at me, Adam Donahue!" But he couldn't help it, and he busted out laughing. She tried to be angry, but adrenaline was racing through her veins and she ended up laughing along with him. Once they got the laughter under control, they took stock of their situation.

"All right, we need to get back upstairs. You good to go?" Adam asked.

She sighed. "I guess. I wish we could just stay here, though." She saw his brows draw together as he got ready to "mansplain" why they couldn't stay so she held her hand up. "I know, I know. You ain't gotta tell me." She lifted the blanket and checked on the baby and dog--both were sound asleep. "We're ready when you are."

They made their way up to the penthouse without incident, and while she made a bottle for

Jayla, who was now wide awake and being entertained by Wylie, Adam rinsed off the pee pad in the shower. They met up in the living room and didn't speak until Jayla was done eating, each lost in their own thoughts.

"I guess it's time to call the cops," she said. Adam nodded and picked up his phone.

"Houston PD? I want to report a missing person and a lost dog. Or, rather, a found dog. I don't know. I just know that somethin' ain't right and we need help."

She watched his expression change as he spoke on the phone. She'd thought she was in love with Jayla's dad, but that had felt nothing like this. This time she was truly, madly in love. With Adam Donahue.

8

"So, is that all? You found a dog who's not supposed to be here, he had something red on his feet, which could've been paint or who knows what, and you knocked at the owner's door with no response?"

"And a strange man has been at the apartment door, twice," Ashanti added.

The officer closed his notepad and tucked it and his pen into his chest pocket. "I understand that might be a little unsettlin', but I'm not seein' anything that points to any kind of crime." As Adam and Ashanti started to argue, he held up a hand. "I'll check on the dog's owner. I'm sure it's just a misunderstanding, but I'll do my due diligence."

As the door closed behind him, she looked at

Adam, tears in her eyes. He looked angry--or maybe, determined.

"Well that's a fine howdy-do. I'm of a mind to report him to his superior."

"I have a better idea." Ashanti's eyes shone and she grinned at him.

"No! We are not investigatin' this ourselves."

"Why not! My uncle's a policeman and your sister-in-law and brother are U.S. Marshals. We got the 'vestigation skills in our blood." She wasn't backing down on this one. If he didn't want to help, she'd do it herself. Even if it meant she had to lug Jayla and Wylie. She knew something bad had happened and someone was targeting Wylie. Strange men had been lurking outside Adam's apartment and she wouldn't feel safe until the mystery was solved.

"Fine then, but we need a babysitter. . .and a dog sitter. I'm not willing to put these two in harm's way. But I won't feel safe until I know that we've solved this mystery.

She jumped back, startled that his words so closely matched what she'd been thinking.

"What?"

"You're a good man, Adam, that's all."

"Well, yeah. You're just figuring that out?" His

smugness charmed her, and she had the strongest urge to kiss him. Luckily, Jayla decided to cry at that moment, saving her mom from embarrassing herself. She held her daughter in her arms and kissed her cheek, while Adam thought.

"I'm going to ask Mr. Cahill if he knows anyone who could watch these two while we snoop around. I trust his judgement and I just don't know anyone else to ask.

"Sounds good to me!"

****

Mr. Cahill suggested he call Mrs. Cahill to watch Wylie and Jayla in the penthouse suite, and Adam gladly agreed. Ashanti was nervous, but within minutes of the woman's arrival, both the dog and the child were enthralled. She was currently sitting in the middle of the floor, on the leopard skin rug Adam had brought from his apartment. Jayla was tucked in the curve of her arm, while she tossed a ball for Wylie to fetch.

Ashanti smiled tenderly at her daughter, who giggled every time the dog dropped the ball in her lap. Mrs. Cahill had thoughtfully brought toys and food for Wylie, which had instantly made them friends for life.

"You ready?" Adam asked.

"As I'll ever be," she replied.

"All right, Mrs. Cahill. You have our cell phone numbers. Call if you need anything. We shouldn't be too long."

She looked up and smiled at Adam. "No problem. These two are delightful; take as much time as you need."

Adam's hand against her back had Ashanti moving out the door before she had time to protest. "They're in good hands," Adam told her, when he saw the dirty look she shot him. "The sooner we figure out what's going on, the sooner we can get back to our own apartment." As soon as the words were out of his mouth, his cheeks reddened, and he looked away. She grinned to herself at his slip of the tongue.

They'd decided to start at Mr. Bedford's apartment and work outwards. They hoped to find a neighbor who'd heard or seen something or find other clues they'd missed the first time. Since they'd called the police, they weren't willing to risk entering the apartment again, at least not without a good reason, so they started with the outside of the front door.

"It doesn't look like the door was forced open, but then again, I broke in without any trouble," Adam smirked. He looked at the ground and whistled. "But lookie here!" He bent down and touched the carpet. "What does this look like to you?"

She leaned forward and nodded her head. "Yep! Them's the same red paw prints that Wylie left in front of our door." They both ignored the fact that she'd said, "our door" instead of "your door." "Are there more? Can we follow them?"

"Oh yeah. They go off in this direction." He led the way, following the bloody paw prints down the hall, in the opposite direction of his apartment. A couple of times he doubled back, losing the tracks, but she pointed out the next set and they were off again. They came to a door marked "Maintenance Only.' The prints stopped about three feet away, and it looked like Wylie had spun in a circle a couple of times. There were more prints leading away from the door and she followed them while Adam tried the door.

"That is one smart dog," she stated as she walked back to him. "He must've been hidin' from someone.

Those tracks lead to a cubby and it looks like he just sat there a while."

"A cubby?"

"You know, one of them places where the wall sticks out then there's like a hidey place behind where the wall goes back."

"Oh, you mean like that recessed area behind the column over there?"

She flapped her hands at him in irritation. "Just forget it. Did you get the door opened?"

"Not yet. It's locked, but I think I can pick it. I didn't want to try until you were here to watch my back."

****

Ashanti stood guard while Adam picked the lock.

"I'm in," he whispered. He pushed the door open slightly and reached in, feeling for a light switch. As the lights came on, he ushered her inside and they closed the door behind them.

The room was full of cleaning supplies, maintenance uniforms, and rows of shelves stacked with cardboard boxes.

"This is creepy," she whispered as she moved down one row of shelves.

"It is kind of creepy," he admitted. "What do you think is in all these boxes?"

"Only one way to find out," she replied, as she pulled a box from the shelf in front of her. She placed it on the floor and opened the top. Inside were personal items; photos in frames, a knitted baby blanket and baby shoes. "What the heck?"

Adam tipped the box so he could read the label. "It says Apartment 716, 2002." He looked up at Ashanti. "I wonder if this is where they keep the stuff people leave behind when they move."

"Or when they die," she whispered, a shiver running through her.

Adam swallowed hard and nodded, closing the box and returning it to the shelf. "Let's look back here."

She followed him down the aisle to the back wall. He stopped suddenly and she ran smack into his back. "What the heck?"

Adam turned and looked at here, his eyes wide. "In the corner. Does that look like Mr. Bedford's missing rug or what?"

She looked over his shoulder and gasped. Against the far wall was a rolled-up carpet that looked suspiciously similar to the Persian rugs in Mr. Bedford's apartment. It was standing on end, leaning against the wall. Someone had pushed a vacuum in front of it along with a milk crate filled with dirty rags. She nodded and grabbed his arm.

Together they moved forward. Adam leaned down and examined the floor. "Ashanti, it looks like blood." He gulped, grabbed the least dirty rag he could see and touched it to the red fluid seeping from the rug. He lifted it and peered at it, then handed it to her.

"Oh, no, I ain't touchin' no bloody rag. No way, no how."

Adam stood up and tucked the rag in his pocket. "I think we need to get the heck out of here and call the police again."

"Fat lot of good that did before. That cop looked at us like we were crazy."

"I know, but this time we've got more to go on. And I've got a secret weapon. My sister Charla is on the force. In homicide."

Ashanti felt the blood drain out of her face. It had just gotten real for her. Until now, she'd hoped they'd find Wylie's owner well and very much alive. As the reality hit her, her knees buckled.

Adam wrapped his arms around her just in time

to keep her from falling. They held each other for a few moments, breathing hard, taking comfort in each other's warmth.

The sound of the doorknob jiggling had them clinging even more tightly to each other as they held their breath, hoping the killer wasn't returning to claim the body. They heard a ringtone and a man's voice say, "Al here. Okay, I'll be right there."

As the man moved away from the door, they both took a breath. Adam loosened his grip on her and they stepped apart, but she wasn't ready to let go. She grabbed his hand and they hurried to the door. Adam opened it a crack and once he was sure "Al" was nowhere in sight, they scooted out into the hallway. Adam led the way to the elevator, and they stood silently, hand in hand, until it arrived.

Mr. Cahill took one look at their faces and his greeting smile was replaced by a frown. "Time to call Charla?" he asked, softly.

Adam nodded and they rode the rest of the way to the penthouse in silence.

9

Adam threw the door open and pulled the petite brunette into his arms.

"Stop it! You're squishing me!" She pulled out of his embrace and shoved him away. "I don't want your cooties on me, you know."

Adam laughed and laid his arm across her shoulders as they turned towards Ashanti. "Sis, this is Ashanti. Ashanti, meet another member of the Donahue clan, my sister Charla."

Ashanti looked down into brown eyes sparkling with mischief. "Hello Charla, nice to meet you," she mumbled, feeling like a giant--an out-of-her-element giant.

Charla smiled and tilted her head to the side as she considered the other woman. "So, this is the woman who's stolen our little Adam's heart." Ashanti felt her face flame and saw Adam's face go bright red as well. "It's so nice to meet you!" She wrapped her arms around Ashanti and hugged her tightly. As she stepped back her face twisted, and she looked at Adam. "I wish it was under better circumstances, though."

He sighed and rubbed his hand across his face. "I just don't know, sis. I want to believe it's a mistake and we're makin' more of this than it is, but my gut says it's bad."

"Well, my guys are checking out the maintenance room as we speak. It could be that this guy just spilled some juice on his rug and put it in the closet until he had time to get it cleaned. Or, I might need to ask you both more questions." She sighed heavily, then looked up at Ashanti, and the smile returned to her face. "Where's this gorgeous baby my brothers keep raving about?"

"She's napping now, but you can take a peek." Ashanti led her to the bedroom where the baby was asleep on the bed, tucked between two pillows, with Wylie curled up next to her.

"Oh, she's precious," she whispered. She looked down at the dog who wagged his tail at her. "And this is the cause of all this hullabaloo, I guess." Her phone rang and she answered, her face serious as she hung up.

"Well, it's official. This is a homicide."

****

"Would you like another cup of coffee, Ashanti?" Adam held the coffee pot in front of him, tilted slightly as if he was pouring it into an imaginary, floating cup. She tried to smile, but her hands were shaking, and her heart was beating fast. He set the pot down and sat next to her, taking her cold hands in his. "It's okay, hon. We'll get through this. We didn't even know him and had nothing to do with his demise. The detectives know that. They just have to ask us about the strange man and Wylie."

"I know, Adam, but it's so scary. I mean, what if that man had busted in your apartment door and taken out me and Jayla? What if Wylie hadn't found us. Would they have killed him, too? I just don't know, I tell ya, I just don't know!"

He leaned in and pulled her against his chest. She could hear his heart beating frantically, but his voice was calm as he replied. "It's okay. I'm here now. And I'm not leavin' you or Jayla or Wylie until this is all over and the bad guys are caught.

She sat back with a skeptical look on her face. "Really? What about your job? This fancy-pants place you live in gotta be costin' you a fortune. Don't you gotta work to pay the bills?"

He laughed out loud, making her scowl. "I've been living alone for a long time. And I make a pile of dough, so the bills are covered, thank you very much. And besides all that, even if they weren't, I'd still stay here with you. I kinda like havin' you around."

She looked into his eyes and saw them shining with love. Love for her. She swallowed hard and swatted him away. "Fine then. You can stay till we're safe again. But then you gotta go back to work."

"Yes ma'am. Will do." He was trying hard to look serious, but at the last minute, his grin broke through and she chuckled.

"All right you two. Ready to be interrogated?" Charla's cheerful voice was at odds to her words, but for some reason, Ashanti wasn't afraid anymore. She needed to share what little she knew so the police could solve the murder and they could get back to their lives. Her breath caught in her throat as she realized she didn't have a life. She'd come here to find a job and a place to live and instead, found herself mixed up in another murder.

"Let's start with you, Ashanti. Tell me everything about finding Wylie. Don't leave anything out, no matter how small. You never know what will break a case wide open."

****

"Well, that was brutal," Adam rubbed the back of his neck with his hand and hung his head down. "Now I know why my sister has the best track record in the precinct. She's like a dog with a bone." They were sitting at the kitchen table while his sister made a call in the living room.

"She's definitely smart and competent. What is it with you Donahue's? How'd you all get to be so wise and good-lookin' and all?"

His eyes sparkled as he lifted his head to look at her. "You think I'm good lookin'?" he asked.

"Not you specifically, I'm just talkin' in general terms here, you know."

He laughed out loud and tilted his head while he thought for a moment. "I think it's just that we had wonderful parents. They loved each other and each of us, no matter what. They read to us, talked to us, explained things to us. They valued hard work, morals and intelligence. And they instilled those values in their children."

"You don't know how lucky you are, Adam Donahue." Her voice was soft and a little wobbly, and he reached out his hand to grab hers.

"Trust me, I do. I think that's another thing they taught us. Be grateful for what you have and don't get hung up on what you don't."

Charla walked back into the room, her eyes landing on their clasped hands. She cleared her throat but couldn't stop the grin that appeared on her face. "We're done for the time bein', but I might need to ask some more questions. One bein', how did you get a pee pad for Wylie so fast. And what happened to the one in Mr. Bedford's apartment?"

Adam looked like a deer caught in the headlights, so Ashanti spoke up. "Mrs. Cahill brought food, toys and treats for Wylie when she came to babysit." She looked Charla in the eye and held her gaze while the woman studied her. It wasn't the whole truth, but it wasn't exactly a lie, so she held onto that thought. The detective smirked and looked over at Adam.

"Anything to add little brother?"

"Nope, I think you got your answer." He grinned at Ashanti and squeezed her hand.

"Ugh. Fine then. I'll let it go—for now. You better hope there isn't any evidence to the contrary, or you'll both be in trouble." She looked from one to the other, then sighed. "I'm tired and I've got a lot of paperwork to do, so I'm leavin'. If you think of anything else, you've got my number. I'll check in with you tomorrow."

Adam stood up and hugged his sister. "Thank you, sis. Drive safe."

Charla waved at Ashanti, then left. And she and Adam were alone.

10

Wylie entered the kitchen, his tail wagging frantically, and headed for his water bowl. "We should probably go to the store and get more food for this dog of yours," Adam suggested.

"He ain't my dog," she countered. The dog in question turned at the sound of her voice and leapt onto her lap.

"He sure seems to think he is."

She laughed as his cold, wet nose touched her neck, and he snuggled closer to her. "Fine then, but he ain't just mine. He's all of ours." As the reality of his situation sunk in, she wrapped her arms around the furry creature and kissed his forehead. "I'm sorry, Wylie. It's hard to lose someone you love."

Adam cleared his throat and she looked up. "Anyone ever tell you you're a good woman, Miss Ashanti Jones?"

She laughed. "Not really, Mr. Donahue. Mostly I been called trouble my whole life."

"Well then, let me be the first. You are one amazin', good woman."

Wylie jumped off her lap, startling them both, as Jayla's coos reached their ears.

"How 'bout I change my daughter and get her ready to go out. I'd like to go to a restaurant tonight, if that's okay with you."

"That sounds wonderful. We can get some dinner and stop at the grocery store on the way back. We can pick up supplies for Wylie and Jayla, and get some pastries for breakfast, too. I'll meet you back here in about 15 minutes?"

"Sounds good." They looked at each other awkwardly for a moment, but Jayla wanted her mom and her cries quickly escalated.

Ashanti walked into the room and picked up her daughter, hugging her tightly. "I love you girl, but you got some timing," she muttered. She knew it wasn't wise to give into her feelings for Adam; but being in this situation had reminded her that you gotta follow your heart, before your time runs out.

She knew Adam was a good man and that he had feelings for her and Jayla. She also knew he was aware of her feelings. She was pretty sure if Jayla hadn't interrupted, one of the other of them would've said something about it.

She got Jayla changed and dressed, then went into the bathroom to freshen up. When she carried Jayla out to the living room, she was surprised to see that Adam had done the dishes and straightened up the living room.

"Is there anything that you don't do?"

"Not that I'm aware of." He grinned and shrugged his shoulders. "I'm just too good to be true."

"Okay, I got it. You don't do 'humble.'"

He laughed out loud and nodded. "That's the truth."

Ashanti handed Jayla to him and went to freshen the water in Wylie's bowl. "We really should get him actual bowls, Adam. This leftover dish was okay in a pinch, but he should have real doggie bowls."

"Sure, put that on the list."

She walked out to the living room where he was putting the baby in her car seat. "Was I 'sposed to be makin' a list?"

"Nah, just a figure of speech. You ready to go?"

"Almost." She bent down and patted Wylie on the head. "You be a good doggie. We gotta go out for a bit and you gotta stay here and hold down the fort. We'll be back soon with some bowls 'specially for you, and some food and maybe even some treats. Okay?"

Wylie yipped and head butted her knees, then ran over to Adam. Adam patted his head and threw a ball across the room.

"Let's go," he said as the dog chased the ball into the bedroom. He pushed the stroller into the elevator and gestured for her to step in. The doors closed just as Wylie came out of the bedroom, dropping the ball as he watched them leave.

"That was mean," she whispered.

"I know, but he would've tried to go with us. And I can't leave him in the car while we have dinner. Plus, it's safer for him here in the penthouse."

They rode the elevator down in silence, Ashanti pondering why she felt guilty for leaving the dog behind.

****

Dinner was lovely and for the first time in days, Ashanti felt relaxed. It had been nice to have dinner with Adam, and the food had been delicious. She'd been worried that Adam would want to eat someplace fancy, but he'd chosen well—a family diner with homemade comfort food.

Jayla had stayed awake for a while, looking around with her big, brown eyes, apparently enjoying the new experience. Ashanti had enjoyed herself, laughing at Adam's jokes and sharing a huge piece of apple pie with vanilla ice cream on top.

After dinner, they stopped to get supplies and she had to rein him in—he really seemed to enjoy buying things for Jayla and Wylie. They got new bowls, a chew toy, dog food and treats for the dog; and more formula, diapers, a bib, and a rattle for the baby.

"How about you?" he asked softly, as she looked longingly at some bubble bath.

"I'm fine. You've already done so much for us."

"Don't be silly. It's been a long day and we all deserve a treat. I'd be happy to get you some bubble bath. I'll even run you a bath when we get home and pour you a nice cold glass of soda, with lots of ice, just the way you like it."

She looked at his smiling face and her heart stopped beating for just a moment. She leaned forward, placing a kiss on his lips. She stepped back, chose the bubble bath she wanted and placed it in the cart. "I'm takin' you at your word, Adam Donahue. I'm expectin' a nice, hot bubble bath when we get home."

As his eyes lit up, she realized how that sounded and quickly amended her statement. "And I expect you to watch Jayla and Wylie while I enjoy my bath."

He grinned wryly and shrugged. "Of course. That's what I was plannin' to do."

They checked out and headed for the car. As they walked through the parking lot, Adam pulled out his phone and started snapping pictures of the sky. "Isn't that sunset beautiful? I wish I had my camera with me."

"It sure is. I love the purple and pink clouds against the dark blue sky." When he didn't respond she turned to him. "Adam?"

He looked at her, his eyes wide. "I knew Wylie seemed familiar to me, and I figured I must have seen him in the building at some point. But now I think I know where I saw him before."

He shoved his phone in his pocket and raced

over to the car. He unlocked the door and reached for Jayla, so he could buckle her into the back seat.

"Come on, Adam! Don't leave me hanging," Ashanti whined.

He stood up and turned around, his eyes shining. "I was out taking pictures the day before I picked you up. I remember seeing Wylie and thinking he looked happy. I took several photos of him and of the people around him."

It took her a second to catch up, but when she did, her eyes lit up as well. "So, you might have pictures of Mr. Bedford, too. And it could help us figure out the timeline of what happened."

"Yeah. I want to get home so we can take a look at my photos. Who knows, maybe they'll help us solve this mystery."

****

Bath forgotten, once they fed Wylie, bathed and changed Jayla and sent her off to slumber land in her crib, Ashanti and Adam sat next to each other at the kitchen table. Adam pulled up the photos he'd taken on his laptop, so it was easier to see them.

Shoulders touching, she watched as he scrolled through to the date he was looking for. From what she saw as he hurried past, the photos were really good. She wanted to tell him so, but he was a man on a mission, determined to find the photos he'd taken of Wylie and hopefully, Mr. Bedford.

"Here we go," he said, whistling softly under his breath as the dog's face appeared on the screen. "This is what caught my eye. He looks like he's laughing, doesn't he?"

Ashanti nodded. "He does, Adam. He looks very happy."

Adam scrolled through the next few pictures and there were several that featured the dog, but none seemed to show who he was with.

"That's weird, I know he wasn't out there alone," Adam mused. He scrolled through a few more, then stopped, leaning forward. "Look. There he is!"

She looked and sure enough, a man was seated on a park bench behind Wylie. The earlier pictures had been taken closer to the dog and the bench wasn't visible until Adam had moved further away. The next few pictures showed the dog playing and the man watching and laughing.

Tears blurred her vision as she looked at the man's face. He'd loved Wylie. It showed. And Wylie loved him. And now, he was gone. Adam sniffled and ran his hands over his face. She was too much of a lady to comment, but she reached for his hand and held it tightly with hers.

"Wait a minute. Adam, can you go back one?"

"Sure. What did you see?"

"I ain't sure, but I think I saw that guy from the hallway."

He scrolled back and enlarged the picture, zooming in where Ashanti pointed. "Good eye, Ashanti, that's him all right."

He went back one more picture, but the man wasn't there, so he went forward. As he scrolled through, they saw the man from the hallway standing behind the bench with Mr. Bedford. In one of the shots, he set a small package on the ground next to the bench. A few shots later, Wylie was sniffing in that area. In the final photo of the dog, whatever had been there was gone.

Adam scrolled forward, but there were no more shots of Wylie, Mr. Bedford or the scary guy. He looked up at Ashanti.

"Are you thinking what I'm thinking?"

"I don't know what you be thinkin', but I'm thinkin' it was never about Mr. Bedford at all. I'm thinkin' Wylie ate whatever was in that package and that's why the bad guy's lookin' for him."

Adam nodded and swallowed hard. "Remember

when you wondered if they'd hurt Wylie if they found him?" She nodded.

As if he knew what they were talking about, the dog jumped up into Adam's lap, licking his face and slobbering all over him.

"I think you need to call Charla."

11

"This is helpful," Charla told them. "I've uploaded this to my team, and they'll run facial rec on this guy. He looks like he'll be in the system. That'll give us an idea of what might have been in that package." She looked over at Wylie who was busy licking himself. "He hasn't um, left any presents we should check?"

Adam snickered and Ashanti replied, "Nope, he hasn't pooped at all. There's been a whole lot of peeing, I'll tell ya, but no poopin'."

"Alright then. Keep an eye on it and let me know. If he hasn't, um, 'pooped' by morning, we might need to take him to the vet and get some help."

"What does that mean? You ain't gonna hurt this here poor doggie, no you ain't!"

"No, Ashanti, nobody's gonna hurt Wylie. The vet can examine him and take an X-ray. If it looks like he's got somethin' in there, he might give him something to help him get it out, if you take my meaning."

She did and she wrinkled her nose at Adam. "Gross."

"What Adam said," Charla confirmed. "Now that you've confirmed the timeline, I think it's safe to wait until tomorrow. If he'd eaten drugs or something it seems like he would've reacted sooner than this. I'm thinkin' it's something solid. But like I said, if he hasn't delivered anything by morning, I'll get him checked out. For now, it's late and we all need to get some sleep."

"Thanks, Charla. We'll let you know. Talk to you in the morning." Adam closed the door behind her and turned to Ashanti. "You never did get to take your bath. Would you like me to get it started for you?"

She saw the fatigue on his face and her heart did a little flip. Even worn out, he still wanted to take care of her. "No, Adam. I'm beat. Let's just get some sleep."

She'd thought it would be awkward, falling asleep with him in the bed next to her, but it had been such a long day that she fell right to sleep—safe in the knowledge that he wouldn't let anything happen to her. And she wouldn't let anything happen to him either. Or to Jayla. Or to Wylie. She fell asleep with a smile on her face, her heart full of love.

****

She woke up to sound of Adam whispering and Jayla cooing. She opened her eyes slowly, not wanting to interrupt the moment. Adam was sitting on his bed with Jayla in his arms. He was telling her a story about Wylie and her, playing in the park. She tried not to make a sound but when he told her daughter not to tell her mama that he took her to the park without permission, she couldn't hold back. She snorted with indignation and opened her eyes.

Adam was grinning at her, a mischievous look on his face. "Took you long enough," he muttered.

"What? Why you tellin' my daughter to lie to her mama?"

"That part was for you, my dear. I knew you were awake."

"Yeah, right," she glared at him.

"You know I would never tell her to lie to you," he said annoyed.

"Haha! Got you back!"

"That was mean, Ashanti Jones. But it was a good one, too."

Jayla realized her mom was awake and turned to look at her. Ashanti sat up and reached for her baby. Adam groaned as he stood up, handing the baby to her mama.

"I'm going to go start some coffee. I have a feeling it's going to be a long day."

"Thank you, Adam," she called out as he left the room. "Don't you ever tell your mama no lies, even if a handsome man tells you to."

"I heard that. You think I'm handsome."

"I didn't say that. I said, '*if* a handsome man.'"

"Yeah right," he chuckled. But then his tone changed. "Oh my! Ashanti, you have to come see this!"

She could hear the excitement in his voice, so she stood up, laying Jayla on her tummy on the bed while she slipped on the robe and slippers. She picked her up and went out to see what the fuss was about.

Wylie was prancing around the living room, a new chew toy in his mouth, while Adam squatted in the doorway of the master bedroom. She joined him and he looked up at her, his mouth twitching with mirth.

"Wylie left us a present, all right."

She looked over at the pee pad and right in the middle was a pile of glittering, shimmering poop.

"What in the world?"

"I'm not positive, but I think Wylie ate the bad guy's diamonds."

****

"Well, that's a new one on me," Charla chuckled as she stood up and removed her gloves. "The lab will have to clean them up, but yeah, it looks like Wylie here ate a bunch of diamonds."

Adam chuckled and patted the dog on the head. "Oh, Wylie."

Ashanti looked over at Charla. "Have you figured out who that goon is?"

"Not yet. The facial recognition software you see in TV shows and movies doesn't exist. The real program takes time."

She was disappointed, but at least they could still hope. It would've been bad if Charla said they couldn't find him.

"What's next sis? We really want to go home. And Ashanti was only supposed to be here for a couple of days. Should I take her back to Stony Gulch?"

She felt her heart constrict at his words and she quickly left the room, not wanting either of the siblings to see her tears. She went into the bathroom, turned the sink faucet on high and had a good cry. Here she'd been thinking that Adam wanted her around while he couldn't wait to get rid of her. What a dummy she was. He was no different than any other man she'd ever met. She was truly a fool.

A tentative knock at the door had her wiping frantically at her face to hide the evidence. "Just a minute."

"It's me, Ashanti. Can I come in?" Charla's voice sounded concerned and Ashanti took a deep breath, then put on a smile, before she opened the door.

"Hey Charla. Did you need the bathroom?"

The woman shook her head, peering at her face. "You left so suddenly; we were worried about you. I just want to make sure you're okay."

"Of course, I'm okay. It's just been a rough couple of days, is all." She tried to smile but she could tell the detective wasn't buying it.

"It's almost over. I got a text saying they found a

match for your bad guy. His name is Elmer Baker. A police unit is heading over to pick him up."

"That's wonderful. Does that mean I can go back to the farm now?"

Charla looked at her closely. "I guess so, if that's what you want. But you haven't had a chance to see Houston, yet. Maybe you can stay a few more days?"

She shook her head. "Adam's right. I'm supposed to go back tomorrow. I have no reason to stay any longer."

The detective chewed her lip, then nodded. "Whatever you want. I'll let you know what I find out."

"Thanks. I think another minute here, if you don't mind."

She stepped back, nodding and Ashanti closed the bathroom door. She sat down on the closed toilet seat and came up with a plan.

****

Adam called out to her from the living room. "Charla called. Those were definitely diamonds Wylie ate. Stolen ones, at that. She said they're part of a jewelry store robbery that went down a few weeks ago. She thinks they were splittin' 'em up to make it easier to transport 'em. Or maybe they were ready to divvy 'em up. Either way, Wylie got in the way of their plans," Adam chuckled.

When Ashanti didn't respond he pushed open the bedroom door. She was lying in her bed with the covers pulled up over her head. "Hey, Ashanti? You okay?"

She didn't want him to see the tear stains on her face, so she pretended to be sleeping. She could feel him hesitate, then he pulled the door nearly shut and walked away. She sighed and wiped her face. She knew she was overreacting, but she couldn't help it. She'd been ready to profess her love for this man and had expected him to return the feelings. But he was ready for her to go back to the farm, so he obviously didn't feel the same as her.

She sat up and held her pillow in her arms, clutched to her chest. Her nana was right. She was a lost cause. She always did this. Adam was a nice guy. He was nice to everyone. It had been silly of her to think just because he was being nice to her it meant he cared about her. What a fool she was!

She sent up a thank you prayer to her guardian angel, knowing she must've been behind the interruptions. Her face flamed as she realized how close she'd come to telling Adam she loved him. Thank you, Angel!

The door swung open and she jumped, but it was only Wylie. He hopped up on the bed and licked her face. "Now doggie, you know I don't like them doggie germs. Keep that licking to yourself."

Wylie listened, for once, and curled up in her arms, against her chest. She wrapped her arms around him and buried her face in his fur. "I'm so sorry, Wylie. It's not your fault, you know. Sometimes we do things without thinkin' and then there's consequences." She looked over at the crib where Jayla was stirring, and sighed. Yep, there were consequences.

She knew she couldn't hide out in the bedroom, but she wasn't quite ready to face Adam, so she picked up Jayla and set her on the bed. She blew air onto her belly, making the baby laugh and Wylie yip. She knew the instant Adam entered the room, and she put on a happy face, so he wouldn't know her heart was broken.

"Hi Adam! Thanks for lettin' me take a little nap. I feel much better now," she said in her cheeriest voice. She turned and looked at him, a big smile on her face.

Adam wasn't smiling. He was looking at her with

concern. She'd better get it together if she didn't want to ruin their friendship.

"I'm sorry I got so weird for a minute. I think it just got to me, is all. But now, I'm back to bein' my normal weird, so it's all good!" He continued to look at her, not saying a word.

Jayla cooed and reached out her hands for him and his smile came back. He walked over to the bed and reached down to grab the baby's hand. "Hi sweetie. Did you have a good nap?"

"Didn't I just say so," Ashanti teased. She stood up and placed her hands on her hips, waiting for him to tease back. But he didn't. He leaned down and placed a kiss on Jayla's cheek, then turned and left the room. She heard the sound of keys and then the swish of the elevator doors closing.

She sat on the bed and lifted her baby into her arms, tears running down her cheeks. He'd left her. He'd done up and left her. And it was all her fault.

12

Maggie's voice was a salve to Ashanti's heart. It had only been a few days, but she'd missed her friend something terrible.

"Hey mama, how's it going out there in the big city?"

"Oh, you know, lots of stuff happening, like murder and finding a dog who poops out diamonds—the usual."

"Yeah, I've heard a bit about your adventures. What is it with you and trouble?" She laughed, but Ashanti felt it hit a little too close to home and felt her anger rise. She needed her friend's help, so she took a deep breath and stayed silent. "Ashanti? You still there?"

"Of course, I am, Miss Maggie, where else would I be?" Her voice sounded strained, even to her ears, so she wasn't surprised when Maggie called her on it.

"Okay, I know that tone. What's wrong and what can I do to help?"

"I don't know, Maggie. I think this has all been a bit too much. I'd like to come back to the farm in the morning, if you or Garrett would be able to come get us."

Maggie was silent for a moment and she could almost picture her friend thinking it through. "Talk to me, Ashanti. What's goin' on?"

"I just want to come home. Is that okay with you?"

"No need to get snippy, you know. I'll have Garrett head out in the morning and pick you up. I'll see you tomorrow."

Maggie hung up and Ashanti felt awful. She's been rude to her friend, even while she'd been asking a favor. Her nana would be so ashamed.

****

She heard the elevator arrive and sat forward on the sofa, waiting for the doors to open and Adam to appear. They slid open and when she saw him, her heart contracted painfully in her chest and she felt like she couldn't breathe.

His face was pale—paler than usual—and his eyes were red. His shoulders drooped and for the first time ever, he looked disheveled. He looked up and met her eyes, then looked away as he walked into the penthouse.

"I was worried when you left without sayin' anythin'. Are you okay?"

"It's been a long couple of days is all. I had some thinkin' to do and I needed to get out of here for a bit."

His tone was cold, and she felt a chill run through her. He walked past her and into the kitchen. She wanted to follow him and ask him what was up, but he didn't seem to want her company, so she stayed put. He walked back out with an iced tea and set it on the table. He sat across from her; his hands clasped tightly in his lap.

"Adam, what's goin' on?"

"I don't know. You tell me, Ashanti. I thought things were good with us, then all of a sudden you started acting like I was invisible. Did I do somethin' to upset you or is this just how you treat everyone who helps you?"

"Excuse me? What do you mean by 'everyone who helps you'?"

"I took you in, you and your daughter, to my home and then you act like you're too good for me, or somethin'."

Ashanti was angry now. He took her in? What was he talking about? "I'm sorry, I didn't realize me and Jayla being here was such a burden. Good to know!" She stood up and he looked up at her, his face tight, eyes wide.

"I didn't mean it like that, Ashanti."

"Then how did you mean it? Cause you just said those exact words to me."

Adam sighed and ran his hand over his face. He looked like he was about to say something, then he hung his head and looked down at the floor.

"Alrighty then. Jayla and me, we'll be gone in the morning and we won't bother you again." She turned and stormed off, ignoring his plea to go back and talk to him.

Even though she wanted, with all her might, to slam the door, she didn't want to wake Jayla, so she shut it quietly. She climbed into bed, clothes on and all, and cried until there were no more tears.

She'd wanted to believe she'd misheard him, that he wanted her to stay, but his words tonight had cleared that up. He didn't care for her—certainly didn't love her, and that was all she needed to know. She'd follow through on her plan, and then she and Jayla could leave Adam and the other Donahues far behind them and start a brand-new life. One without ostrich feathers and white Stetsons.

Having made up her mind, and worn out from crying, she fell asleep. She woke once and looked over at Adam's bed, but it was empty.

****

"Well howdy Ms. Jones and little Miss Jones. How are my two favorite ladies today?" Mr. Cahill's cheerful voice brought tears to her eyes, so Ashanti nodded and turned away, not wanting him to see her red eyes.

They rode down in silence, Mr. Cahill sneaking worried glances her direction. He cleared his throat and softly asked, "Is everything alright, Ms. Jones?"

"It's the way it's supposed to be, Mr. Cahill, and that's what I gotta accept."

He was quiet for a moment. "I'm not sure what's going on, Miss Jones, but I sure hate to see you leaving. You've brightened this place up and me and Mrs. Cahill are proud to call you our friend."

Her eyes filled with tears and she nodded, trying to hold back her sobs. "I 'preciate that Mr. Cahill, but it's time for us to go. We need to find a place where we're wanted, and not a burden on those around us."

Mr. Cahill looked stricken. "A burden? What's this your saying? Who sees you as a burden?"

Ashanti didn't want to speak poorly of Adam or the other Donahues, so she stayed silent, but she could see Mr. Cahill's mind spinning.

"Mr. Donahue cares for you, you know. I don't know what happened between you, but Mrs. Cahill and I saw it with our own eyes. Don't do anything rash, Ms. Jones."

"I thought so, too, but he made it clear that our eyes ain't seein' straight. Thank you for bein' there for me and my daughter, Mr. Cahill. I truly do 'preciate it."

The elevator reached the bottom floor, and the doors slid open. The attendant stood still, uncertain what to do. Ashanti lifted Jayla's car seat higher and grabbed her luggage with her other hand. "Have a nice day, Mr. Cahill. Say goodbye to Mrs. Cahill for me."

He finally realized she was leaving, with or without his help, so he took the luggage from her and strode out of the elevator towards Garrett's truck.

Garrett stepped out and took the luggage from him, thanking him. He looked over at Ashanti and nodded his head. He walked around the truck and opened the passenger door, then placed the luggage in the back seat. Ashanti walked around and handed Jayla to him, so he could buckle her in.

"Hey little missy, we sure have missed you," he cooed to the baby. She grinned and blew bubbles at him, making him laugh out loud.

Ashanti turned and waved goodbye to Mr. Cahill, who looked like he was about to cry, too. Then she climbed into the truck and tried not to start sobbing.

When she got up that morning, Adam had been gone. The key to the elevator was on the coffee table along with a note. It said that he'd been called in to work for an emergency and he asked her to please wait until he got home so they could talk.

She was done talking. She was done trying to have a relationship. She was a mom now and it was high time she got her ducks in a row and stopped living off of other people. When she got the text from Garrett asking if she still needed a ride to the farm, she'd said yes. And she'd been ready when he called to say he'd arrived. There was no point pretending there was a reason to stay—it was time to act like a grown woman and get on with her life.

****

The ride back to the farm was awkward. She knew Garrett had questions, but she didn't feel like coming up with answers. She could see him glancing at her sideways, but he didn't ask. He tried to make conversation, telling her about Walker's new tooth and how Susan and Reed's wedding was coming along, but her throat was tight from trying not to cry, so after a while, he fell silent.

When they arrived at the farm, Maggie was waiting. She threw her arms around Ashanti and kissed her on the cheek. Even though she knew her friend was dying to know what was going on, Maggie let her be, and within a few moments, she and her daughter were settled back in their room.

She laid down on the bed and looked up at the ceiling. She was going to miss this place, that was for sure. If anyone had told her she'd like living on a farm with animals and dirt and stuff, she'd have called them a dirty liar. And if they'd told her she'd fall for a white man with blond hair who liked to dress like Elvis, she would have asked what they'd been smokin'. But both were true. And she was about to leave them behind.

****

Ashanti heard a car pull up in front of the ranch house and decided it was time to come out of hiding. She knew her friends had questions and it was time to give them some answers. When she walked into the kitchen, Susan, Maggie and Garrett were sitting at the table.

"I can't believe the wedding's in two weeks! The time has flown by, thanks to you and Garrett," Susan gushed. Maggie looked over at her handsome husband who smirked, then blew her a kiss. "And Reed is just the most amazing man! I'm so lucky to have found him." Ashanti cleared her throat to announce her presence and when Susan turned, her eyes lit up.

"Ashanti! I didn't know you were back. I heard you had quite the adventure! Tell us all about it."

She sat down at the table and Garrett slid a glass of iced tea in front of her. She looked up at him with a smile of thanks, took a sip, and sighed. It was good to be back, even if it was only for a short time. She grinned at Susan and launched into her story, both women hanging on every word. Thinking about Wylie made her sad. She'd actually grown to love that little doggie. It had been hard to leave him behind, but it would be hard enough to find a place for her and Jayla. She didn't need the added stress of finding an apartment that allowed pets.

"So, this dog ate a bag of diamonds? Is that right? How did the bad guys figure it out? And why did they kill his owner?"

"I don't have all the answers. Charla was still workin' on it when I left. She's a smart one, though, so I'm sure she'll figure it all out."

"So, why did you leave, Ashanti?" Maggie's questions tore at her heart and it took her a moment to be able to answer.

"Because it was time, Miss Maggie. It was just time."

Maggie's face twisted and she looked at Garrett, who shrugged. Susan wasn't quite sure what was going on, so she looked from face to face, then settled for taking a sip of her iced tea. The silent tension was broken by the sound of Walker crying, which was soon joined by the sound of Jayla crying. The two moms grinned at each other, then stood up.

"Is it all right if I get Jayla?" Susan asked. "It's been so long since I've seen her."

"Of course, you can. I'll just sit right here and enjoy this cool beverage." Ashanti grinned as Susan clapped her hands and raced off to get her daughter.

Maggie leaned towards her and said, "This isn't over, Ashanti. I want to know what's goin' on."

She sighed. "I know Miss Maggie. I promise I'll talk to you 'bout it. I just need some time to get my thoughts in order."

Maggie started to say something but thought better of it. As Walker's cries escalated, she shook her head and repeated herself. "This ain't over." She left to get her son and Garrett sat down at the table, across from Ashanti.

"I'm not meanin' to pry, but if my brother did anything to harm you or Jayla, I need to know."

Tears filled her eyes as she looked into his and she shook her head furiously. "No, Garrett, he didn't do nothin' wrong. It's just me. I got some thinkin' to do."

He still looked concerned but accepted her at her word. "Me and Maggie love you and Jayla. If there's anything you need, anything at all, all you got to do is ask."

"I know and I 'preciate that, I do."

Susan entered the room with Jayla in her arms just as Maggie arrived with Walker. Once the babies were fed, the two women moved to the office to finalize the wedding plans. Garrett took Walker out to the barn with him. She'd been surprised when he'd strapped on a baby carrier, but he'd just chuckled. "It keeps my hands free so I can get some work done and he seems to enjoy hanging out with his dad."

Ashanti and Jayla went back to their room for a nap, and she quickly fell asleep. She dreamt of a white wedding with white cake and sparkling white vases full of white ostrich feathers.

13

Ashanti hung up the phone and clapped her hands. Part one of her plan was in motion. Now she had to find some transportation. She'd thought about it long and hard and decided the best thing was to ask for what she needed. She found her friends sitting on the porch swing, iced tea in hand.

"Maggie, could I talk to you and Garrett for a moment?"

"Of course. What's up?"

"Well, I've got an interview at Texas Gold Jewelers and I'd like to borrow your car." At their startled expressions she decided to go all in. "And I'd also like to borrow some money to buy that Ford your neighbor's been trying to sell since I got here."

Garrett looked at Maggie, then stood up. "Anything you need is fine by me. I'm going to go get some more tea. Would you like a glass?"

"I'd love one, thank you."

As he went into the house Maggie patted the empty seat next to her. Ashanti sat down and looked out at the farm. It truly was beautiful here. Peaceful, even. She sure would miss it.

"You gonna tell me what's goin' on or do I have to threaten to shoot you."

"Oh. Miss Maggie. I'm just tryin' to get my life together, is all. I'm a grown woman and I need to be makin' my way in this here world."

Maggie was quiet for a moment, then shifted gears. "I really did miss you," she said, softly. "I'd been so caught up in Susan's wedding nonsense that I felt wore out. But after I told her I needed a break, it was better. The one thing missing was you."

Ashanti wasn't sure she heard her correctly. "You told her you needed a break?"

She laughed. "Yep. I talked it over with Garrett and he suggested I be honest with her. I have to go back to work soon and I was spendin' all my time on the wedding. I wanted to be able to relax and enjoy being with my family and best friend."

Ashanti was stunned. She'd assumed they were talking about her, but it seemed they'd been talking about Susan.

"And then you left for Houston and even though it was only a few days, I missed having you and Jayla here."

She didn't know what to say. All this time she'd felt like she was in the way and wasn't wanted. But it wasn't that way at all. Could she be wrong about Adam, too?

"Maggie, have you talked with Adam lately?"

Her friend turned to look at her, but Garrett walked out just as she was about to answer. "Here you go, ladies. Fresh glasses of iced tea!" He settled onto the chair across from them and looked at her, curiosity shining in his eyes. "I thought you hated that jewelry store. Why would you want to work there?"

"Oh, I don't know. I guess because I'd make money and it wouldn't be as embarrassin' as if I worked cleaning toilets."

Garrett chuckled and nodded. "I can see your point, I guess, although there's nothin' wrong with hard work, you know."

"I know, I'm just pullin' your leg. I want to be a

good role model for Jayla, for one thing. And I want to learn to talk better and be able to make her proud of me. My nana worked real hard all her life and she's still workin' hard. I want to make enough money to take care of me and Jayla and have some left over so I can send it to Nana. You know what I mean?"

"We do, and of course we'll help you. I don't want you driving that heap o' junk Ford, though. We need to get you a decent car if my goddaughter's gonna be ridin' in it."

"Your goddaughter?" Ashanti snorted. "I don't recall that bein' a thing."

"Well, I'm aiming for the title, is all." Garrett grinned. He set his glass down on the porch rail and pulled out his phone. "I think I got just the thing for you. Let me check and see what I can do."

As he stood up, she reached her hand out and grabbed his arm. "I'll pay you back every penny; I swear."

"I know you will, I ain't worried about it." As someone answered on the other end of the line, he walked away, leaving the two women alone again.

"So, I never got to answer your question, but no, I haven't spoken with Adam since you went to Houston. He called last night and left a voicemail for Garrett, but I don't know what he said." She sighed and reached for Ashanti's hand. "You gonna tell me what's goin' on?"

Ashanti sighed and squeezed her hand. "I don't know, honestly. I thought me and Adam had somethin' special. Then he went and said it was time for me to go home. He really hurt my heart, Miss Maggie."

"I've known Adam for years now and I've never heard him tell anyone it was time to go home. Even when it was. Are you sure you didn't misunderstand him?"

"Maybe. But if I did, why didn't he say so?"

"Did you ask him?" Maggie's voice was soft, but direct, and she immediately felt ashamed. He'd tried to talk to her, but she'd pushed him away.

"No, ma'am, I did not. I didn't want to be told I wasn't wanted, so I just left. I just left him and didn't even say goodbye."

Maggie squeezed her hand. "I know that boy cares for you and Jayla. If you care for him, you'll find a way to let him know. And if it's meant to be, it won't be too late."

"But what if it is? What if I done lost him?" As a

tear rolled down her cheek, her friend looked at her sadly, unsure how to answer that question.

****

"I'd like you to meet Ms. Jones, Mr. and Mrs. Compton. She's our newest associate and she's a whiz at finding the perfect piece for every person. If you'll step this way, she'll bring you a tray of rings to peruse." Ms. Morgan gestured to the sitting area with one arm and with the other, shooed Ashanti in the other direction.

She walked over to the counter, stepping gingerly because she wasn't used to wearing heels and her dogs were barking something fierce. She grabbed a ring tray and leaned over the display, looking for rings she thought the Comptons would like. She'd already placed five rings in the velvet slots when Ms. Morgan stepped up next to her to take a look.

"My, but you do have an eye, Ms. Jones. I think they'll love those. No, don't add any more. If you give people too many choices, they tend to get confused."

Stunned by the rare praise, she hustled over to her customers and watched as Mrs. Compton's eyes lit up. "These are beautiful," she gushed, taking a ring from the tray and placing it on her finger.

"That looks absolutely lovely on you, dear," her husband stated, taking her hand and moving it this way and that, making the diamonds sparkle.

"I love it Alfred. I want this one."

As they left the store with the ring in one of Texas Gold's famous boxes, Ashanti felt proud. She'd made a sale and made the customers happy. It was a good day.

"Ms. Jones, may I speak with you in my office?" Ms. Morgan's voice was soft, but Ashanti's heart started pounding anyway. Gregory, the other salesperson snickered and turned away. As she followed her boss, she felt her palms get sweaty. The only time she'd been called to an office was when she got in trouble at school. And her visits to the principal's office generally didn't end well. She followed the woman to the back of the store and sat down in the leather chair while Ms. Morgan closed the door behind them and walked around to sit in her desk chair.

"You've been here for a week now and I have to say, you've surprised me."

Ashanti sat forward and asked, "Is that a good surprise or a nasty surprise you're talking about?"

The woman laughed. "That's what I mean. You've got a sense of humor, humility, great customer service and one of the best, natural instincts I've ever seen. You've done so well this past week that I'm giving you a raise. And a bonus. How does that sound?"

She was flabbergasted. A raise? And a bonus? "It sounds wonderful! I mean, I really 'preciate it, ma'am."

"You've earned it, dear. I wasn't sure it would work out when I met you, but that recommendation from Dr. Slade gave me pause. I figured if he saw something in you, I should give you a chance. And he was right. You really are a marvel."

Ashanti's guts twisted at the woman's words. Dr. Slade hadn't actually recommended her. She'd just said he had, since he wasn't alive to contradict her. It made the words of praise a little bittersweet, so she decided to take the sweet and leave behind the bitter.

"Thank you so much for the opportunity. It means a lot to me. I won't let you down."

"I know you won't. That's all for today, you're free to leave early and spend some extra time with your daughter."

Grateful and still feeling a mite guilty, she just

nodded and headed for the door. She made it out to her car before the tears started rolling. She got a raise! After only a week! Her nana would be proud.

"I'm doin' it all for you, Jayla," she whispered. She started the car and drove back to the ranch house.

14

The next day didn't start off too well. Ashanti got to work early, eager to prove she was worth the raise, but Ms. Morgan was out making special deliveries to her best clients. She and Gregory were there alone, and she felt very uncomfortable. She couldn't put her finger on it, but something just wasn't right with that boy.

She'd already helped several customers and was ready for a break. She wasn't used to standing all day and needed a sit down to rest her tired legs and feet. She looked for Gregory, but he wasn't in the front area. There were no clients in the store, so she walked to the employee area to see if he could keep an eye on the front counter.

As she walked, she heard him talking to someone. She was pretty sure he was on the phone because she couldn't hear the other side of the conversation. At first, she didn't realize what she was hearing. But suddenly, her blood ran cold.

"I told you to find the dog and you still haven't done that. We're not getting paid until I have the dog and the product. Yeah, I realize he'd have gotten rid of them by now, but that dog ruined all my plans to get the heck out of this dump, and I want him taken care of. No, I don't care how you do it, but you'd better find that dog. Or I might have to take care of you, instead."

Ashanti quickly walked back to the front, Gregory's words ringing in her ears. He had to be talking about Wylie. She took a few deep breaths and when he walked up to the counter, she was almost composed.

"Hey Gregory, I was wondering if you could watch the front for a few minutes so I can take a quick break."

He shrugged and nodded. "Sure. Take as long as you need. I won't rat you out to Ms. Mean Morgan." He laughed, but she didn't think it was funny, so she scurried off the back room. She made herself a cup of tea and sat at the break table, thinking hard.

Maybe she was wrong, and it had nothing to do

with Wylie. Surely there was another explanation for what she'd heard. But what if he *had* been talking about him? How was he involved with this whole mess? And who was he talking to? The big, scary guy, Elmer, was in custody. That meant there must be another accomplice.

Her hands itched to pick up her phone and call Adam, or Charla, but she knew she had to play it cool. She needed to get her facts straight. And if Gregory was involved, she didn't want to lead him to Wylie. Or Adam. They'd killed Mr. Bedford. They wouldn't hesitate to kill Adam.

She heard the front door of the store open, and Ms. Morgan appeared, looking satisfied. "That was a productive morning," she announced. She looked down at Ashanti and frowned. "Are you okay, dear? You're looking a bit peaked."

Her guardian angel must be on the job again, because her boss had just handed her the perfect opening! "No ma'am, I'm actually feeling a bit unwell. I was hoping a little sit down and some tea would fix me up, but it isn't helping much."

"Well, you go on home now. Get some rest and we'll see you tomorrow." She left Ashanti sitting there with a big smile on her face.

. . .

****

"Pick up, Adam. Just do it!" Ashanti had called Adam first, thinking she should warn him to keep Wylie out of sight, but he wasn't answering his phone. She'd been sure if he saw her number he'd answer. Maybe she'd been right after all, and he was over her.

"Nope, I'm not assumin' anything," she scolded herself. She hung up and dialed Charla's number.

The woman answered with a brisk, "Detective Donahue here."

"Charla, this is Ashanti and I need to talk to you." She told her what she'd overheard and explained that she was worried it could be connected to the diamond heist. A part of her was afraid Charla would tell her she was crazy, seeing things that weren't there. But Charla didn't say that. She asked her where she worked.

"I'm working at Texas Gold Jewelers."

Charla gasped. "That's the store that was robbed, Ashanti. I think you're on to something."

Ashanti was glad to help but her heart thudded in her chest. "I think Adam and Wylie are in danger, Charla. That Gregory, he wasn't jokin' around. He wants Wylie dead."

"I'm already on it. I'm sending a team to pick up

Adam at work and as soon as I hang up with you, I'll call Mr. Cahill and tell him to keep an eye on Wylie. I haven't been able to get that punk, Elmer, to talk, but now I've got some leverage. Let's see how he responds when I tell him we've got Gregory in custody."

She was confused. "But you don't, Charla."

"He doesn't know that. And I think if he's worried about his brother, I can get him to rat out his accomplice. I don't have enough evidence to do anything about Gregory right now, but trust me, I'll find something, and then this will finally be over.

15

"Adam's safe at Charla's. I don't know how safe Wylie is, though." Garrett chuckled and Ashanti looked at him curiously. "Charla has a Maine Coon. He's an old guy and he's not a big fan of dogs."

She nodded. "My auntie had one of them cats. She called him her sweetie, but he was so big and all, we were scared to go near him."

"Did she say anything about the investigation?" Always the Marshal, Maggie needed more details about what was going on.

"She said that Elmer was singing like a canary. He's blaming his brother Gregory for coming up with the idea and his friend, Jackson for killing Mr.

Bedford. He said they just went there to get the dog, but the old man came home and found them, and Jackson panicked. He said he was yelling at him when Wylie ran out of the apartment and that's when things started falling apart."

Maggie grunted. "I'd say it started falling apart when the dog ate the diamonds. And then again when the guy killed Wylie's owner. But maybe that's just me," she snickered.

"So, what happens now?"

"Charla said they only have Elmer's word about Gregory's involvement, so they're trying to find a way to trick him into admitting it. Or catch him doing something else. She's got the police out looking for this Jackson guy. Either way, she said it's not over yet and she wants you to stay away from the jewelry store until they have him in custody."

Ashanti snorted. "Fat chance of that happenin'. I just got a raise, and a bonus! I told Ms. Morgan I wouldn't let her down and I ain't about to go back on my word."

She expected them to argue with her but instead, they looked at her with smirks on their faces. "What? What's so funny?"

"That's what Adam told her you'd say. Not about

the raise, since he hasn't heard about that, but that you'd rather face a rattler than stand down."

Despite telling herself to stay cool, she felt her chest expand with pride and she grinned from ear to ear. "Dang straight! I want this jerk caught and in jail so we can go back to livin' our lives. And so Wylie can get some justice."

****

"Here, let me do that." Charla bumped the tech out of the way and helped attach the wire under Ashanti's ample breast. "There, how's that feel?"

Ashanti grunted. If she'd known what it entailed to go undercover, she never would have agreed to do it. She had a microphone taped to the underside of her bosom with wires threaded throughout her bra. The earpiece they'd given her made her ear itch and she had to stop herself from reaching up and pulling it out.

Since she'd told everyone in ear shot that she wasn't going to stay away from the jewelry store, Charla had asked her if she'd be willing to help them catch Gregory. She'd watched enough TV shows to know what it meant to go undercover, but now that it was happening to her, it didn't seem so exciting.

Charla had gone over the plan so many times she was sure she'd hear her voice in her sleep for the next month and, although she'd never admit it to anyone, she was scared.

"Okay, one last time, my dear. What's the plan?"

She sighed heavily, then repeated the instructions that had been drilled into her. "We've chosen a time when Ms. Morgan is going to be off delivering jewelry and I'll be alone with Gregory. Any potential customers will be waylaid before they can enter the store and only undercovers will be allowed to enter. If we didn't have any customers, he'd probably be suspicious, so this way, he'll think it's just a slow day. There will be someone keeping an eye on Ms. Morgan, so we'll know if she's on her way back.

"When we're alone, I'll make a comment about how much all the jewelry's worth and say that I wish I could take off with it. If he bites, I'll ask him how he would pull off a jewelry heist, just hypothetical like. Hopefully he'll tell me how they planned the robbery and if he says anythin' specific that only the robbers would know, you'll tell me in my ear and I'll suddenly have to go to the bathroom. Once inside, I lock the door, tap on my wire twice and you'll come in and arrest him."

"Perfect. Now what if he doesn't bite?"

"I go to the bathroom, tap twice and you'll send in two undercovers. Once they're inside talking with him, and he's distracted, I'll go to the back and search his locker. You'll warn me if he heads my way. If I find anything 'criminating, I tap my mike again and you'll come rushing in to arrest him."

"Okay. You've got this Ashanti. I'm confident you'll get him to spill and incriminate himself. And once we have him, things can go back to normal."

"Do you really think so?" she asked, wistfully. "What happens to Wylie?"

"I'm not sure yet. It seems that Mr. Bedford didn't have a will and didn't have any close family. If we don't find someone who wants to claim Wylie, then he'll probably go to the pound."

"Oh, no he ain't. No way, no how! He ain't goin' to no pound! I ain't gonna let that happen!"

Charla grinned. "That's exactly what Adam said." She looked at Ashanti with an odd expression on her face.

"What? What you lookin' at?"

"How do you do that?"

"Do what, Charla?"

"How do you switch from talking with an accent to talking all prim and proper? It's very confusing."

Ashanti straightened her back and looked down her nose at the woman. "I have no idea what you're talking about." She chuckled, then pursed her lips as she thought. "Have you seen Adam in his work clothes?" Charla nodded. "Well, in order to keep that job, he has to play the role. So, he dresses the way he's s'posed to, talks all proper like, and he gives people what they want. But when he's around you or me, he relaxes and lets himself be who he really is. It's one of the reasons he and I get along so good. I'm a big, black woman. Growing up my nana told me that people's gonna see a big, black woman and make 'sumptions, especially if I talk with my accent. She taught me how to talk and act in different situations. When I want to, like when I work at the jewelry store, I can put on heels and a dress and present myself as a professional woman." She paused and took a breath. "Truth be told, it takes a lot of energy and it just don't feel like me. So, when I don't have to, I just don't bother."

"I guess that makes sense. I've always wondered about that with Adam. How he can be so professional one minute, then put on a white suit and strut around saying things like 'y'all' and 'I ain't gonna'." But what you said makes sense. He just wants to be his own self; whatever that may be in the moment."

"See, you *do* get it. I know it don't really make sense, but it's what ties us together. We just want to have a safe place to relax and be ourselves. But we clean up real nice when we have to!"

Charla laughed out loud. "Yes, you do. You definitely do."

The swat team leader strolled over and stood next to Charla. "We're ready when you are."

"Okay, then. Ashanti, you ready to do this?"

Not trusting her voice to sound confident, she nodded, swallowing her fear. As long as Gregory and his accomplice were loose, Adam and Wylie were in danger. Even if she wasn't meant to be with Adam, she didn't want to risk anything happening to him. She would do this for him, and for Wylie.

Charla nodded and spoke into her walkie talkie. "Ready team. It's a go."

****

"Did you see that ring she just bought? Man, I wish I could afford to buy something like that. He paid more for that ring than I paid for my house!"

Gregory grinned and nodded. "I know, sometimes it just doesn't seem fair."

"I know what you mean. Sometimes I just want to scoop up as much stuff as I can fit in my ample bosom and walk right out the door. I wonder what Ms. Morgan would do? Well, actually, I'm pretty sure she would tackle me and frisk me. She's tougher than she looks."

"You have no idea," Gregory muttered under his breath, but the smile on his face made Ashanti pause.

"Wait a minute, no way! You and Ms. Morgan?"

He ducked his head down to hide his blush, but the smile on his face remained.

"How'd that happen?" Ashanti's heart was pounding, and she really hoped Charla was paying attention. They hadn't even considered that Ms. Morgan could be involved.

"I don't know. I guess it's just meant to be." He grinned and she could see he was proud of the relationship. "One night after work she took me out for a drink. One thing led to another and the next thing I knew, I was staying at her place every night."

"I don't know if I should congratulate you or be sick," she laughed.

"I know. It don't make sense. I mean, it *doesn't*

make sense. But she's the best thing that ever happened to me. We'll be able to blow this place, soon, and start a new life together."

Ashanti knew she had to tread lightly, but she really wanted to get him to admit to the robbery. She paused and ran her fingers along the edge of a tray of bracelets. "If I could take just one of these trays, I could start a better life with my daughter. That's all it would take. And it wouldn't be a hardship for the owner, since he's got insurance. You think anyone would miss just one little tray?"

Gregory guffawed. "My woman has an eagle eye. If one ring or even one earring was out of place, she'd know in an instant. She's the real brains behind the operation. Without her the owner wouldn't be the rich old man he is. And yet, he pays her peanuts. It's a shame, really."

"It's so unfair! We're always working so hard and breaking our backs, and for what? To help make the rich guys even richer. And how do they repay us, cutting our hours or changing our health benefits so they can save money." She shook her head. "I wish there was some way to make them pay and get what we deserve."

She kept her eyes on the bracelets, but she knew Gregory was looking at her. She could feel the tension in him and decided to keep her head down and let him ponder her words. It was a good decision because he moved closer to her and whispered.

"What if I told you we've done that?"

She turned so could look him in the eye. "You've done what?"

He swallowed hard and paused, but she could see he was dying to tell her. "We've found a way to get what we deserve and pay that rat-fink owner back for treating us like dirt."

She looked at him and laughed. "No, you didn't. Quit trying to play me." She turned away, hoping she hadn't blown it by taunting him, but no, his pride won out and he couldn't let her snide remark go.

"Yes, we did, I tell ya. It was her idea, but me, my brother, and his best friend, we did the dirty work."

"What are you talking about, Gregory. That makes no sense. Ms. Morgan wouldn't do anything to jeopardize her job. What you been smokin?"

"She did, I'm telling you. She planned the perfect heist. It was amazing, really. And we gave her that, you know, what's it called? When you can't be blamed because you were doing something else at the time?"

"You mean an alibi?"

"Yeah, that's it. An alibi. The three of us robbed

the place while she was at a fancy party. Then we split up the haul and stashed it in a bunch of different places. Only Jennifer knows where everything is. She gave each of us different instructions and we don't know what the others know. That way, she said, if we got busted, none of us knows all the details, so the cops wouldn't be able to confiscate everything."

He was gloating, but Ashanti's stomach was turning. "Wait, so she made you rob the place, then had you hide the goods, but you only know where a third of them are?"

"Well, less than a third, now. My stupid brother lost a bag of diamonds. Idiot. But that's okay, we still got a lot more."

She was pretty sure Charla had enough to arrest him, and Ms. Morgan, but she was curious, and wanted to follow her hunch. "So, then what? When do you get the jewels?"

"Well, that's the brilliant part. She said that we'll lay low till the insurance money comes in. Once they pay it, she'll write a check for the full amount and we'll be out of here, picking up the jewels on the way." He laughed. "That way we get the jewels *and* the insurance money, and nobody will be the wiser."

"Shut up, Gregory."

Ashanti and Gregory jumped at the sound of Ms. Morgan's voice.

"Hey sweetie, I didn't hear you come in. Don't worry about her, she's cool. I was just telling her about our upcoming trip to the Netherlands."

"You fool! You had no right to tell her anything. How stupid are you?"

Ashanti's blood was boiling. Her gut had been right. Ms. Morgan had never planned to take him with her; she just used him to do what she couldn't. She knew it wouldn't be wise to let the woman know she was onto her, so she tried to play stupid. "You're going to the Netherlands? That sounds cool."

"Yep. She told me all about it. I can't wait to go and start our life together, as man and wife."

Apparently, that was too much for Ms. Morgan, because her face twisted, and she looked at Gregory with disgust.

Ashanti couldn't keep quiet any longer. "I don't think she was planning to take you with her, Gregory. I think she was just using you to get what she wanted."

"No way! She loves me. She told me so about a hundred times. Tell her, honey."

Ms. Morgan took a deep breath. "Sorry, Greg, but she's right. You were just a means to an end. You can't actually believe I'd want to be with a man like you?"

****

Even though Gregory creeped her out, it hurt Ashanti's heart to see him talked to that way. She had to remind herself that this was about getting the bad guys and keeping Adam and Wylie safe. He was one of the bad guys and she couldn't blow it now. She reached up and tapped her mike twice, hoping the cops would swoop in before Gregory fully realized he'd been used.

"I'm sorry, Greg, but you aren't exactly up to my standards."

"I don't understand." His voice was tense, and she could see the pulse beating in his throat as he started to realize he'd been a pawn in the woman's chess game. "You aren't taking me with you to the Netherlands?"

She laughed and shook her head. "No, you fool, I'm not. And I'm not going to the Netherlands, either. I have a much better, warmer place in mind. One with no extradition treaty." She pulled a gun out of her purse and pointed it at her former lover. "I was going to leave you alive, but now that you've gone and blabbed, I'll have to kill you both."

The door burst open and SWAT swarmed in. "Hands up! Put the gun down, now!"

Ashanti blew out her breath in a rush and felt her knees start to buckle. She grabbed onto the counter and watched as Ms. Morgan was handcuffed.

Charla had grabbed Gregory and was holding his arm as a police officer cuffed him. He looked at Ashanti with a dazed expression on his face. "I don't understand. She said she loved me. I did this all so we could be together."

As they led the two robbers away, Charla patted her on the back. "Great job, Ashanti! I was worried when Ms. Morgan ditched her tail and showed up unexpected. But you handled it like a pro!"

She felt her chest puff out with pride. "Well, my uncle is a cop, you know. And my best friend is a U.S. Marshal."

Charla laughed. "There is that."

"So, does that mean it's all over?" she asked, her voice sounding a little wobbly, even to her own ears.

"Well, there's still the arrests and trials and such, but yes, Adam and Wylie should be safe now."

"Amen to that," she said as her legs finally gave out and she fell to the floor.

****

Ashanti woke up in the back of an ambulance, a handsome young paramedic monitoring her heart rate and an oxygen mask strapped to her face. She reached up to pull the mask off.

"Hey there, how are you feeling?"

"I got a headache," she said. She reached up and felt the back of her head.

"It appears you fell and hit your head on the floor. You've got a nice goose egg back there."

"I'll say. I don't have no 'cussion or nothin' do I?"

He laughed. "Nope. You don't have a concussion. Just a lump and a bad headache for the next few days. You must have a real hard head."

"You ain't the first person to tell me that," she muttered, making him laugh again.

"Am I interrupting somethin'?"

Adam's voice made her try to sit up, but the pounding in her head made her groan and lay back down.

"No sir. Here, I'll get out of your way if you'd like to talk to her."

The EMT stood up and exited the ambulance, making room for Adam to sit next to her.

He took her hand in his and squeezed it. "Hi."

Feeling shy, she squeezed his hand back, and smiled at him. "Why are you here?"

"Well ain't that a fine howdy-do. I come all this way to see you and all you can say is, 'why are you here'."

She chuckled. "Same old Adam, always gotta make a joke. I thought you were in a safe house or somethin' with Wylie."

"I was—we were. But when I heard this cockamamie idea of yours and Charla's I broke us out and headed over. I got here just before that woman showed up and my sister let me listen in. You were amazing, Ashanti. Truly amazin'."

"Well, it was scary, I must admit. But I couldn't risk anythin' happening to you. I mean, you or Wylie."

"I know what you mean, Miss Thing." He grinned at her, then his face got serious. "I missed you somethin' awful. I don't know what happened, but when we get out of here, could we please sit down and talk like grown folk?"

She nodded, tears filling her eyes. "I'd like that."

Charla climbed into the ambulance. "The EMT

says you're good to go. Maggie and Garrett say they'll keep an eye on you for the next couple of days, so you don't have to go to the hospital. How 'bout we get you home?"

"I'd like that. I need to see my baby girl."

"Can I come, too? I'd like to see Jayla as well."

She nodded. He tried to let go of her hand, but she didn't want to let go. They stood that way until the paramedic cleared his throat. "Let me get you unhooked and then y'all can go home."

16

The next few days were a whirlwind of activity. Ashanti gave her statement to the police and Ms. Morgan, Gregory, Elmer and Jackson quickly turned on each other, hoping to make deals to save themselves. Charla called to say that there was enough evidence to keep them all locked up for a very long time.

Adam had stayed at Stony Gulch Farm and he'd brought Wylie with him, so the little dog had been having the time of his life chasing goats, snuggling with Jayla and Walker, and sleeping alongside Ashanti at night.

Maggie and Garrett had been working frantically to get the farm ready for Reed and Susan's wedding and the big day was almost here.

Ashanti and Adam had tried to talk, but people kept arriving and there was never any privacy. In her heart, she knew that she loved Adam no matter what, but she still wasn't sure how he felt. They'd agreed to talk when the wedding was over and things were calmer, but she found herself in his company more often than not.

"Oh no," Adam groaned.

"What's wrong?" she asked.

"You'll see." He grinned and shook his head. "My brothers are here. Zack and Ack."

"Excuse me? Zach and who?"

He laughed. "When I was little, I would call them Zack and Ack, and the name stuck. They're twins and I thought it was funny. My brother's name is actually Andrew, but I still call him Ack. He puts up with it, but he calls me Smelvis, to get back at me."

"Smelvis?"

"Yes ma'am. Smelly Elvis—Smelvis."

She laughed out loud. "Brothers! He sounds like he's got a good sense of humor."

"Not really. They're both into physical fitness and they run a gym in Rosewood. If you think Garrett and Reed are strong, wait until you see the twins."

Ashanti could hear the anxiety in his voice, and

it touched her heart. "Not all women find muscle men attractive. The one's I've met seem to have traded their brains for muscles. It's the mind and the heart that matter to me."

"That's what you say now, but . . .you'll see."

"Nope. No, I won't. I like what I see here just fine, thank you."

Adam blushed and started to reply, but something caught his eye behind her, and she turned to look.

Adam wasn't wrong. His brothers had muscles for days. They were both shorter and squatter than their brothers, and thick as slabs. She felt the tension increase in Adam as they walked closer.

"Little brother, how's it going?" The shorter one walked over and punched Adam in the shoulder. He laughed and Adam grimaced. She wasn't sure if it was from pain or embarrassment. The man turned to look at her and he grinned. He definitely had the Donahue smile. "Hi, I'm Zack. So nice to meet you."

"Um, you haven't met me, but okay." She looked up at him, a smirk on her face. The other brother laughed and reached out his hand.

"I'm sorry, Zack is a little short on manners. I'm Andrew. And what is your name, lovely lady?"

She smiled up at him and shook his hand. "I'm

Ashanti, nice to meet you," she said, sweetly, earning a grunt from Zack.

Adam stood up and Zack immediately grabbed him in a bear hug. "I swear you get smaller every time I see you." He set his brother down and laughed heartily. He flexed his right arm, showing a huge, bulging bicep. "When are you coming to the gym? Women don't like pale, scrawny men, they like men who look like men!" He flexed his other arm and she'd had enough.

Ashanti stood up and looped her arm around Adam's. "Some women don't think sides of beef are men." She looked him up and down and led Adam away, while Andrew snickered, and Zack looked confused.

****

"Sorry about my brothers. They're an acquired taste."

"That Zack needs a good whoopin', but Ack seemed nice enough."

Adam looked at her, his face twisting slightly.

"Don't get your panties in a twist, I don't like him or nothin', I'm just sayin' that of the two, he seems okay."

"Yeah, well, he was on good behavior today. I'm sure you'll get to see his real colors before the weddin's over."

She stopped and turned to look into his face. "Are they really that bad? Or is this just some leftover childhood resentment 'cause they were bigger and stronger than you?"

He hung his head. "I don't rightly know. They were mean my whole life and they don't appreciate intelligence or hard work. They just want to work out and get stronger. It's hard for me to understand them, I guess."

She placed her hand on his cheek and looked up into his eyes. "If you think it's hard to understand *them*, how do you think they feel? Garrett, Reed and you are all smart, handsome men with important jobs. They spend their time workin' out. That's what matters to them. I'm guessin' they have a hard time understandin' you as well."

He looked thoughtful for a moment. "Maybe you're right. I never thought about it from their point of view. Both of them had a hard time in school. They struggled with their classes. I remember my mom would spend extra time with them going over homework. At the time, I thought they were getting' special treatment. But maybe it was harder for them."

Ashanti grinned and placed a kiss on his cheek. "See, that there is why I prefer Smelvis to Zack or Ack."

He laughed, but as they walked towards the porch, he warned her, "It ain't gonna go well for you if you call me that again, Miss Thing."

She laughed and he held the door open for her as they walked into the afternoon sunshine.

****

Along with Zack and Andrew, the Donahue sisters arrived. She'd already met Charla, of course, but she was nervous about meeting Emma and Bonnie. She quickly found she had nothing to worry about. The sisters accepted her as one of their clan and fell in love with Jayla and Wylie.

"I swear, this little girl is the cutest thing ever!" Bonnie beamed as she held a cooing Jayla in her arms.

"I know, she's my favorite." Reed chuckled as the baby boy in his arms let out a shriek. "Just kidding, Walker. I love you both the same." He kissed him on his tiny nose and was rewarded with a tiny fist in his eye. "Hey, I said I was joking!"

Emma grinned at the hijinks. "Maggie, this place is really lovely. I can't believe how much you've improved it."

"I know! If Garrett was left to his own devices, there'd be a bed, a recliner and a dining table. That's it."

"Yes, but it would be a magnificent bed," he waggled his eyebrows at his wife and she quickly turned red and ducked her head.

"Speaking of beds, it's been a long day and the wedding's tomorrow. I'm gonna give Jayla her bath and get ready for bed myself. It was nice to meet all of you!" Ashanti stood up and lifted her daughter from Bonnie's arms.

"It's wonderful to finally meet you, too. Sleep well and we'll see you in the morning." Emma's glasses slid down her nose a bit, and she absent-mindedly pushed them back up.

Adam was suddenly there, and he reached for Jayla. "Do you mind if I walk you to your room?"

She heard the heavy silence behind her and grinned. This family was nosy, but they cared about each other. "Of course, Adam." The sound of giggling made her turn around, and she saw the happy expression on each of their faces. "Goodnight y'all!"

"Goodnight!"

****

The next day dawned clear and bright and everyone was up early to get ready for the wedding. Ashanti volunteered to watch Walker and Jayla and did her best to keep Wylie out of everyone's way.

She'd hoped to speak with Adam the night before, but when they reached her room, he handed Jayla to her, kissed her softly on the cheek and walked away, leaving her wanting more. This morning he was helping with the set-up and she'd only been able to catch glimpses of him.

She sighed. Weddings were polarizing events, for sure. On the one hand she was thrilled for Susan and Reed. They loved each other and deserved to be happy together. On the other hand, it brought up feelings of loneliness and sadness. Jayla cooed and reached up to touch her mom's face. She smiled down at her beautiful daughter.

She had nothing to feel depressed about. She had Jayla, her friends, and a warm, snuggly dog who loved her. And she'd just helped take down a bunch of robbers. What else could she ask for? As if he heard her thoughts, Adam suddenly appeared and her heart beat faster.

"Good morning! How are my two favorite ladies today?" He bent down to kiss the baby on her forehead, making her giggle.

Ashanti held her breath and he lifted his head, his lips only inches from hers. Would he kiss her, too? He paused looking into her eyes, then stood up. Disappointed, she shifted Jayla on her lap, looking away from the man she loved.

"You look extra beautiful today, Ashanti." She looked up and he was smiling at her, his lips curving gently, yet still too far away for her taste.

"Why thank you. You look hot and sweaty, and not in a good way." She felt her face get hot when she realized what she'd said, but he just laughed.

"It's a good thing I clean up nice," he told her.

She looked up at him, wondering. "You used to work in the barn in a white suit and come back in looking fresh as a daisy. What's goin' on?"

He grinned and shrugged his shoulders. "I don't know. Ever since I met you, I've been all off kilter. You've changed me, Miss Ashanti Jones. Hopefully for the better." He leaned down and placed a quick kiss on her startled lips, then he was gone.

17

The wedding was finally over. Susan and Reed were officially husband and wife and were off on their honeymoon. Most of the guests had left and all that remained from the incredible wedding was the mess. And it was a huge mess.

Maggie sighed. "Remind me again, Ashanti. Who offered the farm for the wedding? And why on earth didn't someone tell 'em it was a bad idea?"

Ashanti put her arm around her friend. "Why, that was you, Miss Maggie. And I believe you had your heart set on it and no 'mount of arguin' would've changed it."

Maggie sighed again. "Darn it, you're right. But look at this mess!"

"No worries, my darlin'. The Donahue clan is at

your service." Garrett walked up behind his wife and placed a kiss on her neck. "We've got this. You two go inside and get a nice, cold glass of lemonade."

Maggie started to argue, but the look on her husband's face stopped her. "Fine then. I won't argue with you. Thank you, love. We'll be in the kitchen if you need us." She grabbed Ashanti's hand and the ladies went into the house.

She poured them each a glass of lemonade, then they sat down at the table. She looked across at her friend. "How you holdin' up?"

"Me? I'm fine. You're the one who did all the plannin' and work. I just watched the babies."

"No, I mean, it's been a long couple of weeks for you. You took down robbers, found a dead body, and through it all remained sane. I would have been cryin' for my mama."

"No, you wouldn't, Miss Maggie. You'd have been brave and strong like always."

"Well, you did your uncle proud, the way you handled yourself out there. Charla and Adam had nothin' but praise for your poise and quick-thinking."

Ashanti looked over at her. "Are you pulling my leg?"

"Of course not? Why would you ask that?"

Maggie sounded offended, but she just didn't believe her.

"Nobody's ever said that I got poise!" She put her hand on her hip and glared at her friend.

"Well maybe not before, but now you got two people who said that!" The two women stared at each other for a moment, then they both started laughing. "Oh man, you know it's been a long day when we get angry 'bout a compliment."

"I'm sorry, but you're right. It has been a very long day." She took a sip of the sweet-tart lemonade and sighed. "And you're right about the last few weeks, too. I hate to admit it, but it threw me."

"You wanna talk about it? About you and Adam?" The words were spoken gently, but she still felt a stab in her heart. She looked into her friend's eyes and she could see the question was sincere.

"I don't know, Miss Maggie. I don't know what went wrong. One minute we were close and the next, he was talkin' 'bout shipping me off back home. It really hurt me, and I didn't know what to do."

"What do you mean, shipping you off back home?"

"He asked Charla if he should send me back to the farm early."

Maggie looked at her with a silly grin on her face. "That's what got you all het up?"

"Well, yeah! Wouldn't you be upset if your man wanted to send you away?"

She sighed and reached across the table to pat her hand. "Girl, you got it all wrong. Adam had texted Garrett to ask if it was okay to bring Wylie with you all. Once Charla started the investigation, he figured it was safer for you to be here. But he said all of you, including him and Wylie."

Ashanti let that sink in for a minute. "But he said he wanted to send me back here."

Maggie took a sip of her lemonade, then asked gently. "Are you sure?"

She thought about it and Adam's words played in her head. *We really want to go home. And Ashanti was only supposed to be here for a couple of days. Should I take her back to Stony Gulch?* "Oh my, oh my. He said 'we.' And he asked if he should take me back. Oh, my word! I got it all wrong. I need to talk to Adam."

****

She rushed outside to where the four brothers and three sisters were putting the yard back to rights. She found Adam and Garrett in the barn, putting away the folding chairs used during the ceremony.

When Garrett saw her face, he excused himself, grinning at her, then left them alone.

Adam turned to see what was going on and when he saw Ashanti, his face lit up. She knew in her heart that she loved him, and he loved her. And it was time for the truth to come out.

She walked up to him, her chest heaving and her breath coming in gasps.

"Ashanti? Is somthin' wrong?" The concern on his face was her undoing, and she couldn't hold back any longer. She stepped closer and put her arms around his neck, pulling his head down to hers, their lips meeting and mingling. His arms wrapped around her and pulled her even closer.

The sound of a truck engine starting brought them back to earth, and they pulled apart just as Charla and Emma walked into the barn. Charla was the first to notice them, and she quickly steered her sister back outside, to give the two lovebirds some privacy.

"I'm sorry, Adam."

He placed his hand on her cheek and stroked it gently. "I'm sorry, too. I don't know what I did to upset you, but I'm so sorry."

She placed her hand over his and looked into his eyes. "I don't know what happened. I don't know if I misunderstood or if it was just my fears of getting' close to you. I ran without givin' you the chance to explain, and that wasn't right."

"None of that matters, as long as we can get past it." He stepped back and looked at her, his face tense. "We can get past it, can't we?"

"I want that more than anythin'. But we have to promise that from now on, we talk first and walk away second."

"Well, how 'bout we talk first and make up second." He grinned and waggled his eyebrows at her.

Ashanti laughed; her heart full of joy. "That sounds pretty wonderful, actually. Can you forgive me?"

"I still don't know what happened, and I need to know. We'll talk about that later, though, when we're not in a barn surrounded by a bunch of nosy Donahues who don't realize I can see them standin' outside the barn!"

Giggles and the sound of footsteps followed his statement, and for once, she wasn't embarrassed. Once things had quieted down, Adam spoke again. "I love you Ashanti Jones. With all my heart. And I love Jayla and Wylie. I'd like us all to be a family, if that's okay with you."

Her heart near to breaking with love, she replied, "Adam Donahue, I'd like nothin' better than to spend the rest of my life with you."

"Way to go, Smelvis!" Andrew's voice rang out. "Woohoo! We got a new sister!" he called out. The sound of cheers and applause made Adam blush.

Ashanti laughed. She was going to have to get used to them. They were going to be her new family.

EPILOGUE

"Are you sure you don't want the job? I'm sure we could find a place to live between Houston and Whitten, so neither of us has a bad commute."

Ashanti had been offered Ms. Morgan's old position at Texas Gold Jewelers and she'd given it a lot of thought. "I really don't, Adam. It was fun for a minute, to be all grown up and professional-like. But truthfully, I just want to spend time with Jayla, you and Wylie. And I want to go back to bein' me."

Adam nodded. "I know what you mean. I just want you to know that I'm okay with whatever you decide. I make enough money for all of us, so you don't need to worry 'bout that. But if you want to do somethin' for yourself, I'm all for it."

She kissed him gently on the cheek and placed her hand over his heart which was beating frantically. "That's one of the reasons I love you."

He grinned and took her hand in his. "One of 'em, huh. What are the other reasons?"

"You're the only man I know who can pull off a white Ostrich feather in a white Stetson."

He twined his fingers with hers. "That's why we fit together so well, Miss Thing. We 'cept each other just the way we are."

"Amen to that," she replied. "I love you Adam Donahue. Or should I say, Smelvis."

"I love you too, Ashanti Jones. But I might have to stop if you call me that again."

She giggled and leaned into his embrace. As he kissed her lips, she could swear she heard her guardian angel sigh with relief.

WHAT'S NEXT?

Read the first chapter of MURDER AT THE MISSION, book 1 of the TEXAS-SIZED MYSTERIES...

I wanted to forgive her; I really did. In fact, I knew that my Poppaw would be disappointed to think I hadn't. I knew that forgiveness would come, but I wasn't there yet. His loss was too fresh, too raw, and seeing her parents at my grandfather's funeral was like salt in that wound, even though I knew that they had done everything in their power to change their daughter's attitude and behaviors.

Poppaw Sewell was known to everyone else as

Pete Sewell, and I do mean "everyone." Goliad is a small town, but Poppaw was extremely well-known and well-loved beyond that. He never met a stranger, and he was always helping others and giving his time, his money, and his love. It was his concern for others that killed him, in fact.

Mariette Jackson hasn't been sober for more than two or three hours a day in 10 years, at least. She bragged that the most work she ever does is to raise a bottle to her glass and her glass to her lips. She races around the county in a bright red sports car – the car changes frequently, since she wrecks them at a rate of about four months or so. Poppaw was behind her on the road that day, with my cousin, Markie, in the truck with him. Markie said Mariette's car was swerving all over the road, and Poppaw had just said that he hoped she made it to her destination in one piece when she veered off the road and crashed into an oak tree.

Markie told us that Poppaw pulled over and jumped out of the truck before she even realized it had stopped. He shouted at her to call 9-1-1 while he tried to get Mariette out of the car; she said he was worried the car would catch fire. Before she finished telling the dispatcher where they were, Markie saw

Poppaw straighten himself out of the car's driver door, clutch his chest, and fall to the ground. She ran over to him, but he was gone. She started CPR, but the doctor told us later that there was nothing that could have saved him – an artery into his big, generous, loving heart basically had a blow-out.

Anyway, I was smiling as best I could, trying to maintain the fiction that I had it together and wasn't seething. Apparently, though, I wasn't doing it as well as I'd hoped. Mommaw Dot came over and sat beside me on the couch, giving me a hug and then placing her hand on my knee.

"You know you have to let it go eventually, don't you?" she said softly.

Tears filled my eyes. "He was a good man. He gave so much to this community, and he died because he was helping a selfish, middle-aged brat who has never contributed one thing to improve the town. Why was he taken from us, while she was left behind?"

"Ssh, Norah," she soothed me. "I don't know the why, but does it really matter? Understanding the reason wouldn't change anything, so dwelling on that part isn't going to make you feel better. And what would your grandfather tell you?"

I tried to resist for a minute, but I finally sighed and slumped back in my seat. "He would say to forgive her, to love her. He would probably quote Colossians 3:13 again."

"'Bear with each other and forgive one another if any of you has a grievance against someone. Forgive as the Lord forgave you." Mommaw winked at me as she quoted the verse.

"Mommaw Dot," I argued, "she doesn't deserve to be forgiven. She's hurt people again and again, although it's never been this bad, and she's never shown any sign of remorse. Why should we forgive her?"

"Again, how would Pete answer you?" She smirked, knowing she had me this time.

I sighed. "He would say that we don't forgive for the benefit of the person being forgiven. We forgive for selfish reasons – that it is a present we give to ourselves. He always said that forgiveness was a sign of strength, not weakness, and that we do it to set ourselves free from the anger and hurt and to find peace." I paused for a second, and then continued. "I know all of that in my head, but my heart can't find its way there yet. I really am trying, though."

"I know, sweetie, I know," she whispered. "You

aren't struggling alone. In the middle of the night, I still feel angry at all of them – at Mariette for driving drunk and having the accident, at your Poppaw for dying, even at Markie for not being able to save him. Then I realize how silly the last two are, and how much the first can hold me captive if I allow it. Those angry moments aren't as frequent as they were, and they pass much more quickly now."

She reached over to the coffee table and picked up a small storage box she'd placed there when she joined me. She held it close to her chest for a moment before handing it to me.

"Your grandfather was so proud of your writing," she said. "He loved you with his whole heart from the moment we knew you were on the way, and that was never dependent on what you did or didn't do. But he loved getting to brag about his granddaughter, the author. We had a conversation about that the night before he died."

She pointed to the package. "For a long time, Pete told me that my parents' story needs to be told. That night, he found me looking through what's in that box. He held me close and said, 'It's time, darling. Everyone involved is gone, so telling the story can't hurt anyone. And, if you ask Norah to write it, you know it will be done well. Talk to her, Dot; the time has come, and she's the perfect person to write it.' I agree with him that the time has come, and I think that the distraction could help you move forward with your forgiving Mariette."

"What story, Mommaw?" I asked. I'd never heard much about her parents, beyond the normal family stuff. "What happened to them?"

"My father, Paul Barger, came to Goliad in late 1935, as a member of the Civilian Conservation Corps camp, to do archaeological excavation and to build the state park. He met my mother there, and, together, they solved a murder that happened at the camp."

"What?!" I exclaimed. "Wow – there's so much there, I don't even know where to start with asking questions! The CCC? A murder? Was he a police officer – is that why he solved the case?"

"No," she smiled at my enthusiasm. "No, he was just a camp worker when one of his cottage mates was killed. Most of the suspects were also his roommates, and there was some question about whether others, including my mother, were in danger. He and Miss Dot talked it over and ended up finding out what happened and why. I think the story would make a great cozy mystery novel, and I'd love it if you are the one to write it."

She tapped the storage box again. "My parents both kept journals all their lives. This box has the ones from the time surrounding the investigation, along with a notebook Grampa used to record notes about what they learned. I think most of what you'd need to tell the story is in there. The rest – the historical part – I'm sure you can find online. Or maybe there's information in the state park archives."

"And what does all of this have to do with forgiving Mariette?" I asked, suspicious of her timing and motivation in passing on the project.

"Mostly, I think it will keep you busy, so you aren't spending too much time thinking about what happened to your grandfather," she answered. "But, I'll admit that I think you'll find some new ideas about forgiveness in their story, as well."

Once again, I sighed. "Okay, Mommaw, I'll check it out. I can't promise that I'll let Mariette off the hook or that I can do a good enough job on the story, but I'm willing to take it on. I'll start reading the journals tonight, and I'll get to the writing as soon as I know enough."

"I'm not looking for promises, *mija*," she smiled.

"And I have no doubt that you'll do a great job. Now, I need to mingle with our guests for awhile." She stood up and started to walk away. Turning back, though, she pointed her finger at me and said, "And forgiveness isn't about letting someone off the hook. It's about letting go of the anger and the resentment – not about removing responsibility."

Later, I didn't even make it across the threshold of my front door before kicking off my shoes. After locking the door behind me, I headed for the bedroom, unzipping my skirt on the way. For this jeans-and-tee girl, six hours in a dress was more than five hours too many.

"Sorry, Poppaw," I called out. "I know the little blue-haired ladies were giving me the death glare for daring to come into the church with bare legs. I didn't mean any disrespect but wearing pantyhose when the heat index is over 110 degrees, I'm not wearing pantyhose for anyone!"

I pulled on an extra-long T-shirt and headed to the kitchen, where I poured a big glass of green tea. I peeked into the refrigerator for something for supper, and I was almost overwhelmed by the wealth of choices. In true Southern style, nearly everyone in town had delivered casseroles, salads, and desserts to my grandmother's and my house.

Mommaw's refrigerator, big deep-freeze, and the extra freezer in her washroom were packed full, and my refrigerator looked like a 3D Tetris game in progress. I also had at least six dishes in my indoor freezer, and there were four cakes and two batches of brownies in the garage freezer.

I pulled out Miz Devereaux's mac-and-cheese and dished some up for the microwave. That woman turned plain cheese and pasta into the food of the angels. To go along with it, I found the tossed salad made veggies fresh-picked from Jerome Fisher's garden.

Just as the microwave dinged, my phone rang. "Shoot!" I said. "Who is calling now? I've talked to everyone in town today; there couldn't be anything else to talk about, and I'm hungry!" I checked the caller ID and couldn't help but smile.

"Hey," I answered the call. "What's up?"

"I just wanted to see how you're doing," Ben replied. Ben has been my very best friend since our church cradle roll days. In the last month or so, we've edged toward taking our relationship in the romance direction. "I hate that I couldn't be there with you for the funeral."

"C'mon, we talked about this!" I said. "When you are the keynote speaker for a state conference, you don't cancel out for anything but your own hospitalization or death. Mommaw and I totally understand why you weren't here, and we're fine with it."

"I know, but I still wish I could have been there to support you," he said. "How did things go?"

"Honestly, it wasn't as hard as I expected," I answered. "I feel like a part of me is missing, but there were so many people sharing wonderful, funny stories about Poppaw that it was easier to get through. I'm tired, though; talking to more people in one afternoon than I usually see in a whole month is exhausting!"

Ben laughed. "And I'm sure some of those conversations were – shall we say – 'challenging'? How many times were you asked when you planned to get a 'real' job, to get married, or to give your grandmother some great-grands?"

"Only once," I snorted. "Minnie Beckrill asked about a job, and Mommaw Dot overheard her. She told Minnie that I had a job that she and Poppaw were very proud of, that what I did or didn't do with my life was no one's business but my own, and that a post-funeral reception wasn't the appropriate place to comment on someone else's life choices. She spoke loudly enough for pretty much everyone in the house to hear her. No one asked anything remotely similar after that."

"Oh, wow!" he snickered. "I wish I'd seen Mrs. Beckrill's face. She must have been shocked to have anyone challenge her right to run everyone's life."

"She looked like a fish," I laughed, "with her mouth opening and closing and her eyebrows nearly to her hairline. When a few people applauded Mommaw's speech, Minnie's face turned red enough to glow in the dark, her eyes narrowed to slits, and she stomped into the kitchen in a huff."

"Well, that took care of the entertainment for the day," Ben said. "Anything else interesting happen?"

I grabbed my supper and settled onto the deep, comfy couch in my living room before answering.

"Well," I hedged. "I don't know if anyone else would find it interesting, but my grandmother did bring something up today. She's not happy that I'm still so angry at Mariette and all that happened, so she offered me a writing project as a distraction."

"Norah, you know she's right about letting go, don't you? I'm not going to lecture you, but I'm a bit worried about it, too. It would be so easy to become bitter over this, and I don't want to see that in you." He paused before saying, "It's the job of a best friend to tell you when you're doing something bad for yourself, right? So, now I've done my job. Tell me about this project."

"She told me that her father and mother met when he was assigned to Goliad with the Civilian Conservation Corps company that built the state park. According to Mommaw Dot, the two of them solved a murder during that time. I'm supposed to write a novel using their story as my inspiration."

"That does sound interesting," Ben said. "Of course, as a historian, the CCC connection interests me by itself, but solving a murder? Was your great-grandfather a law officer or something?"

"Nope," I said. "Apparently, he was working on the construction and on the archaeological excavation. He and my great-grandmother were just amateur sleuths who managed to figure it all out. Mommaw has their journals, and she sent the ones from that time home with me. After I finish my mac-and-cheese, I'm going to start reading them to see if there's enough there. I'm not sure I'm up to writing a full-length book, though. I mean, I've written a couple of nonfiction books, but a novel? I'm not convinced I have a strong enough imagination to handle that much fiction!"

"I have no doubt that you can write it, if you decide you want to," he assured me. "And I might be able to help you with the history part, if you need a little research."

"Well, I'll decide after I read the journals," I said. "Like I said, I don't know if there's enough of the story there to even get me started, but I promised her I'd consider it."

We talked a few more minutes about inconsequential things, then Ben told me that he would be home the next day. We made plans to have dinner together, and I promised that I would have a decision about the book project by then.

By the time I finished my pasta dinner and a generous serving of peach cobbler, it was early evening. I refilled my tea glass and, carrying it back into the living room with me, I turned on the lamp next to the couch and settled in for a reading session.

"Mrr-eow," came from the other end of the room. I looked up to see Tabitha, my Ragamuffin cat, prancing across the floor. She hopped up onto the couch and into my lap, licking my chin before settling in. When I didn't immediately begin cuddling her, she batted my arm and fussed loudly.

"Okay, okay," I said. "Hold on a minute." I stretched my legs and put my feet up on the footstool in front of me, arranged the first journal for reading, and scratched between Tabitha's ears. "You have to be still, though, because I have some serious reading to do."

"Mrrrr," she purred softly, as if to say, "don't ignore me, and we'll be fine."

A couple of hours later, Tabitha stood up in my lap, stretched, and patted my face.

"Not enough attention, sweetie?" I murmured. I looked around the room and realized that the sun had gone down a long time before. I closed the journal I'd just finished reading and carried it to my desk. "Okay, let's get you a snack; it's time for bed."

After devouring her homemade treat, Tabitha sauntered into the bedroom and curled up in the fancy bed my grandmother had bought for her. She mewed a goodnight to me and was asleep almost immediately.

Unfortunately, I wasn't so lucky. I dozed briefly, but then my brain started processing what I'd read that evening. After an hour of tossing and turning and thinking, I gave up. I headed back to my desk, grabbed my laptop, and went back to my bed, where I settled in and starting writing. For the first time in a while, the words came faster than my fingers could type.

What happens next?
Don't wait to find out...

Head to Amazon to purchase or borrow your copy of MURDER AT THE MISSION so that you can keep reading this cozy mystery series today!

YOU MAY ALSO LIKE

Read the first chapter of SAVING SARAH, book 1 of the Gold Coast RETRIEVERS...

Sarah let go of her patient's hand and watched as it settled back on the rumpled hospital blanket. Just yesterday Mr. Hinkley had regaled her with stories of his youthful heroics, of his time spent serving their country in Korea, and of the big, loving family that came after.

For more than eighty years he'd lived life as best as he could figure out how... and now?

He'd died alone in a nursing home, attended only by a nurse and her faithful therapy dog.

Her Golden Retriever whined and nudged the old man's hand one final time before looking to Sarah for guidance.

"Good job, Lucky," she whispered to the dog while pulling herself slowly to her feet. Sometimes she cried when residents left them. Other days she just felt numb. Whatever the particular case, saying that final goodbye never got any easier.

Not for Sarah, and certainly not for Lucky.

"Let's go for a walk," she told the dog as they click-clacked down the hall.

Lucky wagged his tail weakly. They both needed the warm California sun on their faces to coax the life back into them. It was part of their routine—treat, comfort, move on. If they mourned too long, then they wouldn't be on their best game for the other patients who needed them.

And so many needed them.

Each new person who passed through this facility offered Sarah a new life to try on, a new person to become. Outside of her work, her life had been rather unremarkable. She'd always done what was expected when it was expected. She'd gone to school, received straight A's, stayed out of trouble, and treated others with as much kindness as she could muster. Sarah was a good person, but not the kind anyone would remember when she herself passed.

She'd been working at the Redwood Cove Rest Home for the past four years now, and more than three of them with Lucky at her side. Of course, Sarah hadn't originally planned to turn her pet into a colleague, but now she couldn't imagine herself getting through the day without the big yellow fur ball with her every step of the way.

When she'd first approached Carol Graves about adopting one of her famous Golden Retriever puppies, Sarah had only wanted a companion. Once she had secured a degree, a job, and a home, adding a dog to the mix seemed the natural next step. And because Sarah always did her best in all things, she naturally chose the most respected breeder in the entire state.

Carol Graves only bred one litter per year—and only Golden Retrievers. She'd devoted her life to the breed when one such dog had saved her from drowning as a little girl decades before Sarah had even been born.

Most of Carol's dogs went on to work in service, rescue, or even entertainment. In fact, when Sarah had first met the wriggling litter of two-month-old pups, she'd been immediately drawn to a frisky little female who was later named Star. Star now served as a co-host for the local cable morning show. Both Sarah and Lucky enjoyed watching her each day as they ate their breakfast.

But while Sarah had been drawn to Star, Lucky only had eyes for Sarah. Of course, the erstwhile breeder insisted the two were meant to belong to each other—and that was that. Lucky actually came with his name, too. Carol had named him on the day after he was born. She hadn't expected the tiny runt of the litter to survive the night, but he'd surprised her and earned his name in the process.

Lucky had grown into a big, strong adult. No one would ever have guessed he nearly died the same day he was born. Maybe it was that near brush that made him so good with the hospice patients now. He'd been where they were going. He understood and wanted to help.

Which he did. Sometimes Sarah felt as if Lucky was the real medical wonder and that she was merely his assistant.

The Golden Retriever had a knack for knowing which residents were nearing the end, and he made sure they were never without cuddles in their final days. Once they passed on, he switched his attention to Sarah, who felt each loss deeply, no matter how hard she tried to toughen up.

Each death meant losing a patient, a friend, and a life she had tried on while enjoying all the stories and memories—temporarily adopting them as her own.

It was easier that way. Easier than finding her own life and making sure she lived it perfectly.

Just as the breeder Carol Graves had chosen her profession to celebrate a life saved, Sarah Campbell became a hospice nurse to honor the life she'd failed to rescue.

It had been her job to keep her grandmother company that summer day, to help her with anything she needed, and to keep her safe. Sarah had only been fourteen then—far more interested in talking with the attractive twin guys next door than in hearing another of her grandma's rambling stories for the millionth time.

Sarah's selfishness had meant she wasn't there when her grandmother needed help remembering whether she had taken her medication or not. In search of her wayward granddaughter, she'd slipped out of the house and down the front stairs. The ice-slicked steps led to a terrible fall she was just too weak to recover from.

Sarah still remembered the scream. It hadn't been loud and earth-shattering like you'd imagine, but rather meek—a tiny bird letting out a small, shaky chirp as it fell from its nest and crashed to the ground below.

That was the end of one life for Sarah and the start of many others. Yet no matter how many she helped in their final days, she could never quite find a way to forgive herself for letting her grandmother down, for killing the old woman she'd loved with her negligence. Even moving clear across the country, to a place where the winter months remained bright and sunny, hadn't alleviated her guilt. The only relief she had was in doing her best, giving her full attention to those who were left.

Just as she and Lucky had done for poor Mr. Hinkley. They'd done everything by the book. And still... still, she couldn't shake the enormous feeling of disappointment.

As she passed through the automatic doors and headed outside into the facility gardens, Sarah wondered if she would ever have great stories of her own to tell, if her life would ever become more than a vehicle for her heavy guilt, if a change was coming... and if she would welcome it when it arrived.

Finch Jameson had nothing left—no family, no job prospects, and not too much money, either.

Had it really only been five years since he'd been named one of the top thirty business tycoons under thirty?

Yes—five *long* years.

He'd made that list exactly one time before he bought into his own hype and ruined everything. Now, instead of being among the top thirty brightest young minds in the country, he'd become the number one failure, the poster boy for wasted potential.

Growing up, all he had wanted was to take beautiful pictures with his endless parade of yellow disposable cameras. He'd once aspired to be a nature photographer—to see his name in big bold letters plastered across *National Geographic* magazine. Once he hit his teen years, his passion shifted to fashion photography and all the gorgeous models such a career path would bring trotting through his bedroom.

Then, in his second year of college, a stroke of genius took hold of him and refused to let go. With a huge vision and an even more massive team of helpers, Finch brought his big idea to life.

Reel Life.

His fledgling social media network quickly overtook the flashing gifs of MySpace to become the go to place for people to share their lives with the world. Reel Life Finch watched as MySpace Tom sold big and went on to enjoy a relatively anonymous and carefree life.

And he wanted that for himself.

He'd had his time in the spotlight and was ready to travel the world, taking pictures and enjoying every single moment of every day.

He eagerly agreed to sell Reel Life to the first person who asked.

As it turned out, he sold far too soon and for far too little. Seemingly overnight he went from "the one to watch" to the laughingstock of the free world. Luckily, neither of his parents had lived long enough to see his fall from grace. Still, Finch could have benefited from their love and support at the time when all the rest of his friends—and girlfriends—had abandoned him.

With nothing left, he abandoned LA to settle in the small coastal town of Redwood Cove. The money went fast, mostly due to a string of poor investments and bad advice.

"Why don't you just come up with another idea?" everyone asked.

But Finch was fresh out of brilliant inventions. Reel Life had been the pinnacle, and now at thirty-one years old, his life was already on the decline. His blazing passion for photography dulled to the tiniest of sparks buried within a giant mountain of dying embers.

It was all just too painful, too much of a reminder of what he'd not only lost but willingly given away.

Somewhere in the midst of yet another day whittling away at the time between waking up and going back to sleep, a letter arrived.

Not an email, but an old-fashion letter scrawled carefully in large looping cursive.

Dear Finch, it read, *I'm your great aunt Eleanor, and I'm dying. There's something very important I need to tell you before I go. Please come see me at the Redwood Cove Rest Home. I pray this letter finds you well... and before it's too late to set things right.*

Regards,

Eleanor Barton

Finch read the letter three times over before folding it back up and slipping it into the torn envelope. A great aunt? No, that was impossible. His mother loved celebrating what little family they had. She wouldn't have let them grow estranged from one of the few surviving relatives.

He'd never once heard of the Bartons. Why would this sickly old woman reach out to him? How could she have gotten her wires so badly crossed? Made such a huge mistake?

He had half a mind to crumple the letter and toss it in the trash. This clearly wasn't his problem. But then again...

His imagination conjured a withered old waif of a woman staring forlornly out the window waiting for her lost nephew to return to her side. Could he really let her die thinking her attempt to mend fences had been met with cold refusal?

He didn't owe this woman anything, but he also couldn't live with yet another burden on his conscience. It was bad enough he'd tossed his own life in the crapper. The least he could do is help this sweet old lady find her family.

One good deed for the day, then he could return to his lackluster life.

Head to Amazon to purchase or borrow your copy of SAVING SARAH so that you can keep reading this romantic suspense series today!

ABOUT THE AUTHOR

Michelle Francik is the author of three books in the Texas Sized Mysteries sub-series, The Donahue Brothers of Texas. She writes from the heart, creating realistic characters and charming dialogue, hoping to bring a little mystery, romance, and laughter to your day.

She lives in South Lake Tahoe with Oreo--a mysteriously charming cat who likes to help her write by sitting in front of her computer monitor, so she can't see the screen.

MORE FROM SWEET PROMISE PRESS

ROMANTIC SUSPENSE

The Gold Coast Retrievers

Six special Golden Retrievers help their humans solve mysteries, save lives, and even find love...

CONTEMPORARY ROMANCE

The No Brides Club

When six friends make a pact not to let love get in the way of their careers, the No Brides Club is born. But could the right man at the wrong time cause them to break their vows to each other?

The Celebrity Corgi Romances

Meet six Corgis who live the high life as celebrity BFFs. One thing's for sure: When their people fall in love, it better be with someone who loves dogs as much as they do!

The Sweethearts of Country Music

Six musicians come together to form an all-girl country band. But when love comes calling, will the ladies be able to balance their musical worlds with their romantic lives?

Holidays in Hallbrook

Welcome to Hallbrook, New Hampshire. A small-town filled with the unexpected, lots of love, and of course, a beloved dog to ramp up the excitement. Home is where love leads you.

Mommy's Little Matchmakers

For these moms, a second chance at love may need a "little" extra help.

First Street Church Romances

These sweet and wholesome small town love stories with the community church at their center make for the perfect feel-good reads!

HISTORICAL ROMANCE

The Pioneer Brides of Rattlesnake Creek

Their fortunes lie out west...and so do their hearts.

Sweet Grove Historical

Go back in time to follow the lives and loves of Sweet Grove's founding families in this historical romance series.

COZY MYSTERY

Pet Whisperer P.I.

Glendale is home to Blueberry Bay's first ever talking cat detective. Along with his ragtag gang of human and animal helpers, Octo-Cat is determined to save the day... so long as it doesn't interfere with his schedule.

Little Dog Diner

Misty Harbor boasts the best lobster rolls in all of Blueberry Bay. There's another thing that's always on the menu, too. Murder! Dani and her little terrier, Pip, have a knack for being in the wrong place at the wrong time... which often lands them smack in the middle of a fresh, new murder mystery and in the crosshairs of one cunning criminal after the next.

The Funeral Fakers

Professional Mourning can be a deadly business. Luckily, these 6 out-of-work actresses are on the job!

Texas Sized Mysteries

The stars at night are big and bright, deep in the heart of Texas... but so is the trouble. These cozy mysteries feature characters who are larger than life and cases just begging to be solved by any reader clever enough to rise to the challenge.

Made in the USA
Columbia, SC
26 March 2020